# RUMOURS AND ROMANCE

## JULIA JARRETT

Edited by CM Wheary

Book Cover by Shanoff Designs

Special Edition Published 2023

# CONTENTS

# Chapter One

*Mila*

The best part of owning my own bakery is getting up before dawn to bake.

I'm serious.

There's something so peaceful about being awake before anyone else, turning the lights on in my kitchen and seeing the clean countertops gleaming, just waiting to be covered in flour and sugar. Pretty soon, the smell of yeast will permeate the air as the bread proofs, cinnamon and spice will overlay it once I get the muffin batter mixed, and maybe today I'll finally find the time to experiment with the savoury loaf I want to try for sandwiches. Sundried tomatoes, oven roasted garlic, and asiago cheese.

Yes. Please.

The next hour is spent listening to my favourite true crime podcast and mixing up different batters and doughs. By the time my assistant arrives, I've got three batches of our famous apple nut muffins in the oven, and enough bread proofing for the two dozen loaves we normally sell in a day.

"Hey, Mila," Kelly comes walking through the back door, hanging her bag on a hook and going immediately to the sink to wash up.

"Morning, what's on the cookie menu today?"

I'm a good baker. I don't say that to be arrogant, I say it because it's the truth. Yet for the life of me, I cannot bake a decent cookie. I'll follow a recipe, yet they end up hard as hockey pucks. I'll try to freestyle something, and they're soggy piles of mush. Kelly, on the other hand, is a verified cookie-making wizard, creating flavour combinations that I could never think of in a million years. When I hired her, I told her that her responsibility was to save the citizens of Dogwood Cove from my cookie disasters. She laughed, until she tried one of mine. There was no looking back since then. We make a good team, and I'm considering offering her a manager position soon.

"Mmm, I'm feeling salty today. Salted caramel chips in dark chocolate, and peanut butter — both versions, with and without chocolate chips."

My mouth is already watering. "Make sure you save a salted caramel one for me, okay?"

"You bet."

We fall into our routine, working side by side. I'm focused on mixing up some bran muffins, what I affectionately call *geriatric muffins* seeing as they're popular with the older residents of Dogwood Cove. I don't sell a lot of them, but I try to keep at least a dozen around most days. After that batter is ready, it's on to blueberry banana muffins, and then I can start the scones.

Eventually, the rest of the team arrives — one more baking assistant and my morning cashier. The sign gets flipped to open, and the second-best part of owning my own bakery can begin. I always spend the first hour going between the kitchen and the front of the bakery, greeting my regular customers and enjoying their reactions to whatever we've baked that morning. Food equals happiness, and I love seeing that.

"Mila, girl, give it up. What is *in* these scones? They are incredible."

I glance up from the glass case where I'm restocking the apple nut muffins and smile at one of my favourite customers.

"Hey, Riley, glad you like them. I got some real maple syrup and wanted to experiment. What do you think? Do maple bacon scones meet your standards?"

Riley maneuvers her wheelchair around to the edge of the counter so we can chat more easily. "I want to marry this scone, Mila, seriously."

"Don't tell your husband that," I tease. "Or maybe you need to take another one home to Dean."

"But if I share, that will mean less for me."

I shrug and give her a sly grin. "Then take two more and eat one before you get home."

Riley lifts her hand up for a high five. "Now you're talking."

I reach into the glass case and pull out a couple of scones, putting them in a bag and handing it to Riley.

"Whatever happened with that guy you met in Westport?" she asks, opening the bag and sniffing deeply. "Oh my God, that smells so good."

I rest my elbows on the counter with a small groan. "He was an idiot. Can you believe he actually admitted he was moving back home with his mom, and I quote, 'so he could spend more time mountain biking and less time working'. Seriously, where are the guys with a work ethic? With a career? Goals? Anything remotely resembling maturity." I shake my head as Riley laughs. "I'm serious. No more dates. I'm just going to focus on the bakery from now on."

"I'm sorry, girl. You really do have shitty luck with men. Maybe if you weren't so amazing, it would be easier to lower your expectations."

"No way. If my mom taught me anything, it was to never settle."

Riley waves her hand in the air. "Amen, sister. On that note, I guess I need to get home to Dean. We're meeting with the fertility specialist later."

My eyes widen. "Oh my God, that's so exciting!"

I haven't seen Riley this happy since her wedding day three years ago. With her spinal cord injury, pregnancy is probably going to be a challenge. But I know she and Dean will be incredible parents.

"It really is. Okay, I gotta go! See ya later."

I watch as she wheels herself out the door. Riley does have a point, my standards are high. Too many casual relationships and failed dates with guys who just couldn't live up. But I've got a great life by myself; I've got goals, and dreams, and I want a partner who can handle that. Not someone who's going to whine every morning when I get up before dawn, or hold me back from doing what I want.

Because I'm watching Riley leave, I can't help but notice who walks in right after. *Hello hottie.* This guy has that perfectly styled brown hair that looks messy but you know actually took some effort. He's staring down at his phone, so I let myself shamelessly stare, feeling my heart speed up. That surprises me; it's been a while since a man intrigued me like this one does. I take in his strong jaw, covered in a dusting of scruff, and eyes that are far too serious for this early in the morning. He's tall, broad shouldered, and wearing a crisp mint green dress shirt, tucked into dark grey pants, both of which are fitted to his body perfectly and show off what I'm certain are some incredibly drool-worthy muscles. But the over-the-top professional look seems completely out of place for both my bakery and the town. We're more of a jeans and T-shirt kind of place. Even my brother, who happens to be our mayor, gets away with his plaid shirts and denim. His girlfriend, who's also my best friend, calls him 'lumberjack' for that very reason.

But this guy's city boy appearance doesn't stop the fact that I feel like the air in the bakery just got sucked out around me. He is *that hot.* My eyes blink rapidly and I force my thoughts away from the very dirty path they were traveling down, just in time to give him what I hope is a welcoming — and not too lascivious

— smile. But before he can say anything, my damn mouth runs away from my brain. See, I tend to have an instinct about what kind of muffin or treat someone needs when they walk in the door. Sometimes I say nothing, and let them choose what they want, but sometimes I blurt things out without thinking.

"You need a maple bacon scone."

His eyebrows rise up in surprise at my outburst.

"Thanks, but I'll just take a black coffee and..." — his eyes quickly scan the display case — "a bran muffin."

A geriatric muffin? No way. He's way too sexy for that, but my brain kicks in and I remember he's a stranger, not a local. I manage to keep my mouth shut and my eyes focused on what I'm doing instead of on his muscular forearms that are revealed by his rolled up shirtsleeves.

I now know what those romance books my friends and I are hooked on mean by forearm porn.

"Umm, okay. Sure. Sebastian can ring you up. Have a great day," I hand him the bag with his muffin and gesture over to the cash register before bolting back into the kitchen.

That was weird. I'm not the kind of girl who gets flustered over a guy. As much as I might complain about the lack of handsome men in town, I'm not actually interested in dating right now. My sights are set higher than love. Although, watching my best friend Summer fall for my brother, Ethan, has been pretty incredible.

But while they've been making heart eyes at each other, I've been looking into expanding the bakery into the space that's available next door. Until recently, it held a small art studio. Ethan and I own the building, thanks to our inheritance from our parents and Ethan's smart thinking about property investment, but that space has always been rented out. Now it's empty, and the dream my mom and I shared of expanding beyond just baked goods into a lunch spot might be realistic. Which means no time for hot guys with sexy forearms.

I didn't think about the hot guy and his boring bran muffin for the rest of the day and even more surprisingly, I didn't mention him when I met up with Summer and our other friends, Paige and Serena, for book club. Which, let's be honest, is more of a chance to just sit and drink wine and eat snacks than actually talk about the book we read. But Paige, who owns the bookstore on the other side of my bakery, insists on calling it book club, and also insists on giving us discussion questions each month. We rarely get past the first one or two questions.

My head is pounding when I open the bakery the next morning, courtesy of too much wine and not enough sleep. But I still settle into my routine and before long, muffins are baking, bread is proofing, and I'm rolling out cinnamon buns.

When the bakery opens, I wash my hands and head out front. After chatting with a few of the regulars, I turn to head into the kitchen and grab another tray of muffins from the cooling rack. When I go back to the front, Summer is there, chatting with Sebastian, who is back manning the cash register again this morning.

"Tell the truth, you smelled the muffins from upstairs, didn't you?" I tease as I load the tray into the display case, taking one out for her. She's living in the apartment above the bakery, and comes here for breakfast most mornings.

"Maybe, but I'll never admit my addiction to your baking." Summer's blue-green eyes dance with happiness. I love having her back in town. After eighteen years, she came home this spring to deal with her late father's estate, which included a run-down beachfront resort just outside of town. We've all been trying to help her get it cleaned up, but without a serious influx of cash, I worry whether she'll be able to get everything done.

"Well, let me send you off with something extra." I add in one of Kelly's cookies, and hand the bag over to Summer. "I might be able to swing by the resort later this afternoon if you want some help."

Summer takes the bag from me and dismisses my offer with a wave of her hand. "Nah, it's okay. I'm not going to do too much today, and your brother already promised to come by and help later. Why don't you enjoy an afternoon off? You work too much."

She's not wrong, I do work a lot, but it's because I love it. And because I made a promise to my mother after she died that I would make our plans a reality. The Nutty Muffin would be more than just a bakery, it would be a café serving breakfast and lunch, all with my homemade breads and rolls. That's why, for the last five years, I've done nothing but work every day, investing in rental properties with my brother and busting my ass at the bakery for ten hours or more each day. Because every penny I can earn and save is a step toward my dream.

Still, a couple of hours to myself sounds glorious. And I can't remember the last time I went kayaking.

"Fine. I know when I'm not wanted." I wink as she goes to pay.

"Bye, Mila. Have some *fun* today."

I turn back to the kitchen, and check that everything is okay. A tray of bread loaves is ready to go into the oven, so I pull on some heat resistant mitts and load it into my industrial-sized oven. When I go out front again, *he's* back.

And just like last time my stupid heart speeds up, my mouth goes dry, and my hand, which is likely covered in flour, goes up to twist a piece of hair around my finger like some silly schoolgirl with a crush.

"One bran muffin and one black coffee. That'll be three seventy-five, please."

Sebastian hands over the man's order and takes his money. And I stay partially hidden and ogle as those delicious forearms reach out and take the change offered to him. It's a real shame that someone so handsome eats such boring food. Before my curiosity can get the better of me, and make me ask him who he is and why he's punishing himself with bran muffins and black coffee, when there are cinnamon buns and lattes in the world, he's gone. Leaving me even more intrigued by the sexy visitor to Dogwood Cove.

Several hours later, I'm back in my car after going for a paddle around a lake located an hour inland. Kayaking is one of my favourite activities, and being out on the water today made me realize just how long it's been since I went out by myself. I'm feeling refreshed and energized, despite only getting five hours of sleep, and I have to admit, Summer was right to push me to do this.

I'm driving down the highway, windows rolled open and music blaring, when I see a dog limping along the side of the road. I slow down and pull over. There are no properties around here, just forest, so I have no idea where the dog came from, but it's definitely hurt. I walk closer to it cautiously, holding my hand out.

"Hey, puppy. Who's a good dog? Are you okay?" I keep my voice soft, and I watch its ears perk up when it sees me. There's no collar, but the dog comes to me easily, sniffing and licking my hand. "Well, you certainly are a friendly thing." A glance between the legs tells me he's a boy. "Okay, boy, I can't leave you here. Think you want to go for a ride?"

The dog limps over to my Jeep, then stands there looking at me. "Crap. You can't get in, can you?" A low whine melts my heart and I give him a boost into the backseat. "Okay, I got you now, buddy."

I take the rest of the drive back to town a lot slower, glancing in my mirror every couple of minutes to look at my passenger.

He's lying on the back seat, tongue hanging out, and I swear he looks like he's smiling. He's huge; must be a lab mixed with something big is my guess. The problem is, what do I do with him now that I've got him? Dogwood Cove doesn't have an animal shelter, so I phone the one in Westport, which is the closest town to us. When they say they're full and can't accept him, I'm stumped. The next closest place would be Victoria, but that's over an hour away. "We'll go see Ethan. He'll know what to do." The dog lets out a low ruff of agreement. At least, that's what it sounds like to me.

But when we get to Ethan's office, he's in the middle of a crisis, thanks to his idiotic decision to keep a massive secret from Summer. I can't help him get out of this one, and he can't take the time to help me figure out what to do with the dog. Which makes our next stop the local vet clinic.

When I park out front, I turn back to the dog. "Okay, buddy. I hope you're not one of those dogs who's scared of the vet, because we need to get you checked out. And you're a lot bigger than me. So let's do this together, okay?"

He hops out of the back seat, landing on three paws. I'm worried about that leg of his, which is crazy, seeing as he isn't even my dog. But I feel responsible for him. We head inside without any issue, and I check in with the receptionist. A few minutes later we're in the examination room, waiting for Doctor Morton, the town vet.

"Mila Monroe, what have we here?"

Doc Morton is an older man, with one of those loud booming voices that always startles me. When I jump at his voice, the dog lets out a low gruff, and leans into me. My hand goes to his head and I scratch his ear.

"I found him on the highway. He's limping, and there's no collar. I figured my first stop should be to get him checked out."

"That was a smart idea, Mila. Let's take a look."

Even though Doctor Morton's specialty is large animals, like horses, he does a thorough examination, and I'm impressed by the fact that the dog sits patiently through it all. His soulful brown eyes — the dog's, not Doctor Morton's — are on me the entire time, and I feel myself becoming more attached every minute. Wherever this guy came from, he seems like a total sweetheart, and I can't imagine a family not missing him. But he doesn't have a tattoo or a microchip, and the receptionist couldn't find any dogs like him listed anywhere as missing, which leaves his appearance on the highway a mystery.

"Without doing any more intensive diagnostics, I would say his leg was injured somehow. Maybe he was hit by a car; we'll never know. But the good news is that rest, gentle activity, and some anti-inflammatories should help. You can either take him to Victoria or hang onto him for now." Doctor Morton removes his gloves and leans back against the counter. "I'm not sure if we'll ever figure out who his owner is or was. But he'll need to go somewhere that can manage his limited mobility and make sure he gets the medication for his leg daily."

I nod slowly, my eyes cast down at the dog's head that is resting on my lap. "I'll take him home for now."

"Okay, let me set you up with some tablets to get you started, and a list of what you'll need from the store. Next time you come in, I'll have you meet our new veterinarian. I believe he has some more recent experience treating orthopedic injuries in large breeds."

And that's how I find myself loading the dog back into my car and heading to Westport, where there's one of those big pet stores. I'm several hundred dollars poorer, but the dog has been vaccinated, had x-rays of his legs done, and pronounced healthy, except for the leg injury.

Later that night, after dealing once more with my idiot brother and his royal screw up with Summer, I climb into bed and turn on my side to watch what the dog does. He ambles over to the dog bed I placed beside my own, and sniffs at it. Then he turns three times before collapsing into a pile of furry limbs.

"Good night, pup. We'll figure out a name for you in the morning." I yawn, my eyes closing after what's turned out to be one hell of an eventful day.

But my last thought before I fall asleep isn't of the dog asleep on the floor, or on Ethan and Summer's fight. No, the last thing that runs through my mind is, I wonder if I should make bran muffins tomorrow morning.

# Chapter Two



*Jackson*

If you had told me six months ago that I would be moving to a small town on the coast of Vancouver Island to try and become partner in a local vet clinic, I would have laughed in your face.

But that was before. Before my ex-fiancée decided to come clean about lying to me for five years. Before my former boss at the animal shelter was caught embezzling funds that should have gone to the animals we were caring for. Before my life imploded and I needed to get away from it all.

Truthfully, just one of those two situations would have been enough to make me want a fresh start. But together, they spelled disaster if I stayed in the city. So when I saw the posting for a small clinic in Dogwood Cove that read *future partnership opportunities available* I applied. And here I am, sitting in a motel room with my cat Harley curled up on the bed, scrolling through house rental listings.

When I look at my watch and see I've got two hours before my meeting with Doctor Morton at the Dogwood Cove

Veterinary Clinic, I decide to go and get some breakfast. The bakery I walked into the first morning I was here comes to mind. More specifically, the woman behind the counter who tried to convince me to order some crazy scone or something. I feel a slight frown furrow my brow, remembering the look of disappointment that crossed her face when I declined, choosing my standard breakfast instead. Ten years of a protein shake first thing, and a bran muffin with black coffee after a workout is a hard habit to break, and I wasn't about to do so on my first day in a new town. Too much change is never a good thing.

I pull a pale blue pinstripe shirt out of the closet and put it on over my bare chest. Harley lifts his head to fix me with his yellow-eyed stare. "I have to go to work now. We'll find a house soon with a sunny spot for you." A scratch to his head, and a shake of my own for talking to my cat, and I'm out the door.

The nice thing about this town is how close everything is in the downtown area. The motel is a five-minute drive from the bakery and the vet clinic is just down the street. I could walk, but it's a warm June day and I don't want to be sweaty when I get to the clinic. Doctor Morton asked me to come in early today to finish our discussion about my goals and plans, which I hope will include more details about the partnership opportunities he lured me here with.

Pushing open the door to The Nutty Muffin bakery, I am assaulted by the aroma of fresh baked goods and coffee. Even I can admit it's a tempting combo. I wait in line, and when it's my turn, I place my order, trying not to be too obvious about looking around for the woman from yesterday. Not that I have any interest in pursuing something; dating is the last thing on my mind right now. But any man could see she was gorgeous in that classy girl next door kind of way. Long brown hair tied back in a braid, curves in all the right places, and a warm and inviting smile. The exact opposite of my ex, Stefani, who embodied the ice queen look from her platinum hair and willowy figure to her cool blue eyes.

I take my coffee and muffin and climb back into my car. A few short minutes later and I'm parked outside the clinic, where I quickly eat the muffin, which I have to admit is a lot better than any other bran muffin I've ever tasted. Once I've checked my shirt for crumbs, I get out, grab my coffee and my satchel, and head inside. I give a nod in greeting to the vet tech and receptionist as I head to the back-office area, where I deposit my bag and grab a set of scrubs to change into. If I remember correctly, I've got a dental cleaning and two neuter surgeries to do today, while Doctor Morton handles the regular appointments.

The man in question comes into the office just as I'm reviewing the chart for my first patient.

"Ah, good morning, Jackson. Lovely day, isn't it?" He puts his bag down and claps a hand on my shoulder.

I look up with a professional smile. I'm not quite as outgoing with my greeting but try to sound friendly "Doctor Morton. Nice to see you, sir."

"Enough with this 'sir' business, I told you to call me Phil."

I nod and go to sit in the chair in front of his desk as he settles in behind it. "Phil. I'm eager to continue our conversation from yesterday about the opportunities for me here."

"Yes. We'll get to that. First, how are you enjoying the town?"

I try to curb my impatience. If he wants to waste time with small talk, I'll play along. "It's a beautiful area. Very different from the city. I'm going to get out on the water this afternoon, and I'll be viewing some rental houses tomorrow."

"Rental?" Doctor Morton scoffs. "You should be investing, my boy. Owning real estate is the best way to get established in town."

This is similar to the tone of our conversation yesterday. I get the feeling he wants to know I'm here to stay, but making a commitment to something, even a house, feels like too much for me right now. After all, the last commitment I made started with a diamond ring and ended with a broken heart.

"I'm sure I'll do that in the future," I say, hoping it's enough for now.

"Hmm. Yes. And have you had the chance to meet anyone?"

For fucks sake, what is this, a matchmaking interview or a professional discussion? I decide to try and steer the conversation toward what I'm hoping to hear. "I haven't had much of an opportunity yet. Speaking of opportunities, I would be curious to hear some more about what you meant by potential partnership opportunities. As you know, that was a driving force behind my applying for the position here." Hopefully my blunt approach works.

"Ah, yes. I suppose I should elaborate further on that." He leans forward and steeples his hands on the desk. "The wife wants me to slow down my work over the next few years. That, and as you know, my specialization is really in large animals. We've got more hobby farms popping up in the area, and the demand for veterinary services for those animals is increasing. My hope is to secure a partner who can take over the majority of the domestic animal practice in town, freeing me up to both take on the large animal work, and lighten my overall hours."

I nod, trying to curb my enthusiasm. This is exactly what I've been hoping to hear. But when I open my mouth to respond, Morton keeps on going.

"You've never lived in a small town, Jackson, so forgive me if this sounds patronizing. We're a close-knit community. People here want to know who they're trusting their animals to. They want to know you. Anyone who becomes a partner in my practice will become an integral part of the tapestry that makes up this town. I need to know that you're committed to Dogwood Cove for the long haul, that you see yourself making a home here."

I get it. He wants me to say I'll stick around, that I won't leave for another opportunity in a couple of years. The problem is, I have no idea how to prove to him that won't happen. I can say I have no intention of moving, I can tell him — again — how making partner in a clinic is my career goal, and this opportunity meets all of my requirements. But I'm starting to suspect he wants something more tangible. The problem is, I don't want to buy a house right now, I have absolutely no intention of starting a family, or anything else that would prove I'm settled. For now, my words will have to do.

"I appreciate that, Phil. And I am committed to staying here. I hope we can revisit this conversation in a few months when I've shown you that commitment."

After a second of silence, he nods. "Right, then. That sounds like a plan. Now, shall we review what's on the docket today?"

A few minutes later, I'm heading into the surgical suite to scrub up and get ready for my first procedure of the day. My mind is so focused on the stats of the animal coming in, a ten-month-old yellow lab named Tucker, that I don't notice the person walking toward me until we collide.

"I'm so sorry," I say, my hands automatically coming to a set of slender shoulders. My eyes meet green ones, lined in heavy black liner, and I mentally curse and drop my hands instantly. Of all the people it could be, it had to be her. Veronica is one of the veterinary technicians, and yesterday when I was introduced to the team, there was no mistaking her open appraisal of me. When she asked if I wanted to get a drink after work, it only confirmed to me that she was not so subtly hinting at being more than just friendly to the new staff member. Dating someone I work with is an absolute non-starter, even if I was interested. Based on the way she's batting her eyelashes at me, she's probably hoping my hands on her body wasn't the accidental impulse it was.

"It's no problem, Doctor Holt," she says with a high-pitched giggle that instantly grates on my nerves. "I'm scrubbing in with you today, won't that be fun?"

I make a noise of acknowledgment as we both walk the rest of the distance to the surgical suite. Once there, I tune everything out, going through all of the steps to prepare for the procedure. Another tech has Tucker ready, so I quickly wash up, pull on a scrub cap and gloves, and take my place. Veronica comes to stand beside me, too close beside me, and I sidestep away.

"Everyone ready?" When the two techs nod at me, I begin. It's a simple and quick procedure but I take it seriously every time I have an animal under anaesthetic. My attention is focused on Tucker, and I execute his neutering flawlessly.

Half an hour later, I'm washing my hands in the sink when Veronica comes up beside me again. I stifle a groan of frustration.

"Your hands were so...talented, Doctor Holt." Good God, the sexual innuendo is dripping from every word this woman says. It's uncomfortable and I'm wondering how the hell to make it clear to her I am not interested in anything more than a professional acquaintance.

"Thank you, Veronica. I appreciate your assistance." I keep my tone formal, and immediately leave to phone Tucker's owners to assure them the procedure went well.

Somehow I manage to avoid Veronica for the rest of the day, and by the time I'm off, she's already gone. I head straight back to the motel, feed Harley, and spend a few minutes with him.

My body is full of energy that needs to be released, so I grab my paddle board, change into my swim shorts and rash guard, then load up my car and follow directions to the beach. The ocean is calm, and there's only a few people around. As soon as my feet hit the sand, I feel myself calm. Water has always centered me, and there's nothing more peaceful than being out there on my board, feeling the burn of my muscles working to stabilize myself and move through the water. I zip up my life jacket, and head down to the water's edge. It's cold, but I don't plan on getting wet today. I zip my phone into the waterproof belt pack I carry, which also holds my keys and a water bottle, and push off from the beach. Staying on my knees, I paddle out for a while before standing up. My board slices through the water, and instantly everything inside of me settles. My mind empties of stress, and I leave it all behind for a while.

An hour of strenuous paddling later, I can feel my muscles starting to shake, so I turn back toward shore. When I reach the beach, I lay my board down against a log and sink down onto the sand. It's warm from the sun that's been shining all day, and being this close to the dinner hour, the beach is mostly empty. I close my eyes and let myself think about the last time I was out on the water. It was the day after Stefani dropped the emotional bomb on me that she wanted kids, and if I didn't, then she couldn't marry me. To say her ultimatum came out of nowhere is an understatement. For the five years we were together, I thought we were on the same page. She had made it clear she was fine not having children, that she loved me, and wanted to be with me no matter what. Then one day, she comes home and announces that she had been lying, hoping I would change my mind, and that having a family was important to her. And if I wasn't willing to give her a family, then I clearly didn't love her enough and the wedding was off. The problem is, I've never wanted kids. And she knew this when we first started dating. I'm happy being the fun uncle to my two nieces and one nephew. So I called her bluff, not thinking she was serious. But the diamond ring still sitting in a box in my suitcase says she was.

The paddle I went on the next day was fueled by heartbreak and betrayal. I thought she was the woman I would spend the rest of my life with, and it turned out our entire relationship was built on a lie.

Today, being on the water felt like the last step of my fresh start. It might be the same ocean, but here, there is an entirely different energy.

# Chapter Three

*Mila*

I decide to call the dog Milo.

Yeah, Mila and Milo. We're quite the pair.

The last several days have been a whirlwind, from getting Milo settled, all the normal life stuff that happens when you own your own business, to dealing with my dear old brother being a total idiot and almost screwing things up with Summer. The last required me to step in and help him think of a way to fix everything. All of our friends pitched in to help Ethan set up an amazing surprise for Summer down at the resort she now owns, which I don't regret in the least, even if it did mean longer days than I normally have.

I haven't seen the bran muffin man because I've been so busy in the kitchen playing catch up, but Sebastian assured me he's been in every morning. I'm pretty certain my employee has a bit of a crush on the man, and I don't blame him. But Bast is happily dating someone, and much to my embarrassment, he noticed my ogling the other day. Which is why he's loving being able to rub it in my face that I've missed the hot man for four days in a row.

Tonight is my weekly dinner with Ethan, and now Summer joins us, too. I'm taking Milo with me, of course, which I'm sure my brother will just love.

Sure enough, the frown he gives me when I walk through his front door makes the obnoxious little sister in me do a happy dance.

"Seriously, Mills? You brought the dog?"

"His name is Milo. And yes, I did, he wants to meet Auntie Summer."

My brother just rolls his eyes, but I notice how his hand goes to pet Milo's head.

"Oh my God, he's huge." Summer stops where she is, walking out of the kitchen with two glasses of wine in her hands.

"Is one of those for me? Gimme, gimme," I gesture to one of the glasses, and she hesitantly walks over and hands it to me.

"Mila. That thing is massive."

"That thing," I say primly, "is your dog nephew, Milo. He's a gentle giant, I promise, and the only nephew you're gonna get."

We go to the back deck, drinks in hand. I let Milo off his leash and he lumbers down to the grass, his limp making me frown, before flopping onto his back and rolling around. I watch affectionately, loving how relaxed and happy he seems, despite his leg.

"You got a dog. And you named it Milo."

I turn to my best friend who's sitting beside me, watching Milo's antic, with a smile on her face as well. I knew she would love him.

"Thanks for stating the obvious."

Summer smacks lightly at my hand. "Don't be a brat or I'll start calling you Mills."

I pretend to shudder, even though I'm pretty sure Summer knows I love the nickname my brother uses for me. "You wouldn't dare."

Her wicked smile tells me she might.

"Okay, ladies. Dinner is served." Ethan walks out with a platter piled high with grilled chicken and sets it down on a table already filled with salad, grilled asparagus and fresh bread — from my bakery, of course.

"Looks great, big brother." I grab a plate and start piling on the food. I've got a healthy appetite, and my brother is one hell of a cook.

At some point during dinner, Milo wanders over and lies down between my chair and Ethan's. Of course, I notice him casually slide a piece of chicken down to my dog, but I don't draw any attention to it. For all that he wants to give me a hard time about taking in Milo, Ethan's an animal lover just like I am.

"At least this dog means you've got some protection at home," my ridiculous brother says, making me roll my eyes.

"He's a lover, not a fighter."

Summer touches Ethan's shoulder, and looks over at me. "What your overprotective brother means is, we're glad you're not alone."

I take a deep breath. "Look, guys, I was alone for a long time before I got the dog. Nothing's changed. Besides, it wasn't that long ago that you two were alone as well." I fix them both with a pointed stare. Summer has the decency to squirm; Ethan just stares right back.

"It's different, Mills. You can't tell me you don't get lonely sometimes; I know how often you would show up here to watch TV."

"Maybe I just wanted to hang out with my brother. Is that a crime now?"

Ethan leans back in his chair and puts his arm around Summer. "Of course not. I just want you happy, that's all. And doing more than just work and sleep."

"You just said I watch TV."

"You know what I mean, Mila," Ethan fixes me with a frown.

"Just because you two are love-drunk happy doesn't mean everyone needs to be. I'm perfectly content with my bakery, my family, my friends, and now my dog."

Thankfully, they don't push me any further, and eventually the conversation drifts to the resort that Summer is updating. Her grand reopening is just a few weeks away, and we're all getting excited. Her dad leaving the resort to her in his will was sad, naturally, because he died before they could reconcile. But I can't ever be upset that it brought my best friend back to town.

Having her fall in love with my brother was weird at first, but it's all worked out.

Amid talk of furniture and landscaping, I start yawning. Not because I'm bored, but because my early morning is catching up to me and I'm ready to head home. The downside of opening the bakery every morning is that I need to be in bed by nine. With a container full of leftovers for my lunch tomorrow, I hug my brother and Summer goodbye, and Milo and I drive the short distance back to my house.

Pulling into my driveway, I turn off the engine and sit there, looking at my house. I love it, don't get me wrong. Ethan and I decided our first investments with the money our parents left us would be houses for ourselves. It was a smart decision, and over the years I've made it into the perfect home for myself.

At least I thought it was perfect for just me.

Maybe it's the conversation from earlier, but suddenly I'm struck by how big of a house it is for just one person, with three bedrooms and a large yard. I have no intention of having kids, but still, rattling around the place does get a little lonely. Not that I would ever admit that to Ethan and Summer. With Milo here, some of that has abated, and the yard is now full of tennis balls and rope toys. But talking to myself every evening has turned into talking to my dog, and I'm not sure which is more pathetic.

The next morning Milo and I arrive at the bakery before the world wakes up, as usual. He settles right down on the dog bed I set up for him over by my small desk area, and promptly falls back asleep. Lucky dog. I turn on my podcast and get to work mixing up dough, and setting loaves that proofed overnight in the oven. Over the next couple of hours, each of my staff arrive, and the day starts humming along perfectly.

Right before I switch the sign to open, I go outside to the sidewalk in front of the bakery. Turner and Pete, two of the older men in town are waiting patiently. They're always first to arrive, and sit over a cup of coffee and a scone each morning. I greet them, then put down the full bowl of water I've always supplied for the dogs in town. Having Milo makes it all the more meaningful to me. Back inside, I wander through the space, making sure the cushions on the chairs are fluffed, and everything is clean and cozy looking. A smudge on the front of the display case catches my eye, and I quickly wipe it away. No smudges allowed.

Half an hour later, I'm running the cash register while Sebastian is busy helping Riley and her husband, Dean, with their order when the door to the bakery opens, and in comes bran muffin man. His eyes widen ever so slightly when he sees me, but he doesn't answer my smile with anything more than a small nod of his head.

"Good morning." His voice rumbles over me.

"Good morning, back for another geriatric muffin, or can I interest you in something else this time?"

Finally I see his lips quirk up at the corner. "Geriatric muffin?"

"Yup. I only make the bran muffins because they're popular with the over sixty crowd. You're the youngest person to order one in months."

He raises his eyebrows at me, but there's a slight smile on his face. "Well, sorry to disappoint, but I'll take a bran muffin and a dark roast coffee, please."

I let out a small huff and roll my eyes, softening it with a smile. "Fine. But one of these days, you've got to try an apple nut muffin. I'm famous for them, you know."

He inclines his head toward me. "I did not know that. Congratulations."

"Thanks. I mean, I'm only famous here in town, so I guess it doesn't count as much. But still, that's why the bakery is named The Nutty Muffin. Get it?"

Oh Lord, Mila, shut up right now.

But his eyes are dancing at my rambling, even if his face is still fairly stoic. This guy is a tough nut to crack, pun intended. I pass him over his muffin and fill his travel mug with the coffee he requested.

"Are you staying in town?" I'm being nosy, as per usual. He cocks his head and pauses a second before answering brusquely.

"Yes, at the motel for now."

Geez, the guy doesn't believe in small talk, I guess. He turns to go, and I call out one last thing, determined to have the last word.

"See you again tomorrow."

He pauses halfway to the door, turns back to me, nods once, and then he's gone. And I have a new mission. Somehow, I will make that man smile. And eat a cinnamon bun.

That afternoon, I leave the bakery early and take Milo back to the vet clinic for his follow up. Doctor Morton wants his new vet to assess Milo's leg, and I have to admit that my own personal curiosity has me excited to meet the town's newest resident.

But nothing could have prepared me for when the door to the exam room opens, and bran muffin man walks in. The white lab coat over his button-down shirt is weirdly sexy, and the look of confusion on his face might just be the most expression I've ever seen from him.

"Hi." I give a small wave, feeling ridiculous.

"You're Mila Monroe? And" — he looks down at the chart in front of him — "Milo? You named your dog Milo?" His voice is layered with surprise.

I cross my arms and fix him with a glare. He had better not be mocking my dog's name. "I am and I did. I assume you're the new vet? Or do you just like to tease people about their pet's names?"

He closes his eyes briefly, and when he opens them again, I'm disappointed to see a cool veneer of professional distance obscure his face. "Apologies. I meant no disrespect Miss Monroe.

I'm Doctor Holt." He puts out his hand and I move to shake it. His grip is firm, his hand warm, and strong. But he breaks contact after only a few seconds to drop down into a squat on the floor and greet my dog. Before I can warn him that Milo likes to sit on people, my giant dog has knocked him off his feet and climbed right on. And then, a freaking miracle happens. Bran muffin man laughs.

"Well, hello big boy," he says, ruffling Milo's fur with a smile. He starts to run his hands over Milo's body, and my dog is soaking it all up. Doctor Holt looks up at me with a far more professional expression than he's showing my dog. "Doctor Morton told me you found him on the side of the road, and you've decided to keep him?"

"That's right." I sink down onto the chair, and Milo gets up and comes over to me. His loyalty makes me smile. Doctor Holt stands up and brushes off his pants.

"Have you had a dog before, Miss Monroe?"

His question is curious, not judgmental, and I detect the smallest of smiles as he watches Milo leaning into me.

"I have. We grew up with dogs and other animals. And you can call me Mila."

His eyes flash up to mine, and there's a look of, dare I say, interest there. But it's gone in an instant.

"Alright, Mila. I'm glad to hear you have some experience with dogs. Owning one is a lot of work; I would hate to have Milo with someone who didn't appreciate that. Now, Doctor Morton mentioned he had started Milo on some anti-inflammatories for his leg injury. It's a bit soon to see much of a result but have you noticed any difference?"

"To be honest, I don't know. The day I picked him up is the day we saw Doctor Morton, so I don't really know any different from how he is now."

He nods, his gaze thoughtful and focused on Milo. "Understandable. Let's see how he walks."

I stand up and Milo dutifully walks with me up and down the length of the room. I try to see if I think his limp is any better, but really, I can't tell. After, Doctor Holt does some more assessments, moving Milo's joints gently, murmuring softly to him the whole time. His warm demeanour toward my dog is so at odds with the cool, formal vibe he's given me so far. It's weird, but I want to crack that shell and find out who this guy really is.

"What's your first name?" I blurt out.

He looks up at me in surprise. "Oh. Ah, it's Jackson." His brow furrows slightly. "Sorry, I'm not used to being on a first name basis with patients."

I wave his apology off. "No big deal. We're just friendly like that around here. And since you know my name, and you eat my muffins, it felt weird calling you Doctor Holt." As soon as the words leave my mouth I blush, realizing how awkward they sound.

But once again his lips quirk up in a slight smile, relieving me of my embarrassment. "Right. Well, you can call me Jackson. And your muffins are...delicious." And then, he winks. *Winks!* The action is so at odds with the cool demeanour he's shown me so far that I can't help but laugh. Milo gives out a bark and nudges me with his nose, and soon Jackson is chuckling with me and the whole energy of the room changes. Gone is the formal, standoffish approach, and in front of me is a man who is relaxed and friendly.

I lean back in my chair as Milo goes back over to stand by Jackson. His hand drops down automatically to scratch the dog's head.

"Now that we're on a first name basis, I have to ask. Why the bran muffin every morning?"

His cheeks darken and for a minute I worry I've become a little *too* friendly. Damn. What if he has like, digestive issues and needs the fiber. Oh my God, I do *not* need him to start talking about his bowels.

"Forget I asked, it's not my business. I'm just nosy."

"It's just habit. Back in college, I would work out in the morning, then grab a muffin and a coffee before class. The only place on campus that was open early enough had disgusting muffins. All except their bran muffin. I've had one every weekday morning ever since."

"Well, that's disappointing," I comment, and he barks out a laugh.

"Why?"

"I was hoping there was some good story. Not just, habit. Then again, at least you didn't start talking about your fiber intake." I shudder comically and am rewarded with another chuckle from Jackson. "But if it's only a habit, it should be easy to change. Next time you're in, I get to choose what you order."

He watches me, and for a minute I think he's going to refuse. But then his shoulders lift, and he smiles. "Deal. But I'm keeping the black coffee."

A few minutes later, Jackson walks Milo and I out to the front. There's two women there, the receptionist who checked us in, and Veronica Garrett. Ugh. We went to high school together, and to say we didn't get along is an understatement. We were constantly trying to one-up each other in class and out of class. She may have been head cheerleader, but I came away with valedictorian. I forgot she worked at the vet clinic. Great, hopefully I don't have to deal with her too much.

What's really interesting is the way she reacts to seeing Jackson. I see her eyes light up, and not in a good way, and swear to God, she tugs her scrub top down to show off more cleavage. But when she reaches up to touch his arm, he pulls his arm away by reaching into the jar of dog treats and coming around the front of the counter to give one to Milo.

"It was great to meet you both," he says, giving me a warm smile as he pets my dog. Behind him, I see Veronica narrow her eyes at me, and I barely hold back my grin of triumph. That's right, bitch, he's friendly to me.

"Yeah, thanks for checking him over for me."

"Of course. If I think of anything else that might help, I'll let you know, but for now we'll just wait and see if the medication helps." Jackson gives Milo one more pat to the head, then turns to go to the next patient, successfully dodging Veronica by going around the other side of the desk. I give her a wave of my fingers as I leave, but once I'm outside, I free the snort I've been holding in. Honestly, I feel kind of bad for Jackson if she's got her sights set on him. She's relentless, and something tells me he will need to figure out a way to shut her down, and fast.

# Chapter Four

*Jackson*

Thursday is my favourite day at the clinic. For the stupidest reason.

Veronica doesn't work on Thursdays.

The last two weeks have become increasingly awkward as she continues to try and flirt with me. It doesn't seem to matter how many times I step away, or try to respectfully decline her invitations, she just keeps trying. Doctor Morton even witnessed one time when she had her hand on my arm and was leaning way too far into my personal space, and when I moved away from her, I saw his frown from across the break room. How the hell do you tell your boss that your coworker is hitting on you inappropriately and that you have zero interest in reciprocating?

But waking up today, still in the damn motel because I haven't found a rental that I like yet, but knowing I won't have to put up with Veronica's advances, has me smiling and whistling to myself in the shower.

Or maybe it's the fact that Mila promised to make lemon blueberry scones this morning. My mouth waters just thinking about them. Somehow, that woman has managed to convince me to give up my ten year habit of a bran muffin and black coffee for whatever fruity, sweet concoction she mixes up. Over the last two weeks I've had her apple nut muffins three times — they're that good. Cinnamon buns, raisin scones, banana chocolate chip muffins, and some crazy Italian pastry I can barely pronounce. She's a wizard in the kitchen, and is turning into a decent friend as well. At least that's what I tell myself is the reason I've gone into the bakery every single day these last few weeks. Every day that is, except Sundays. She doesn't work Sundays, so I don't bother going. And no, I don't want to think about why that is.

Sure enough, when I push open the door to The Nutty Muffin an hour later, Mila looks up from behind the counter with a warm smile.

"Perfect timing. Scones are cooling and we just made a fresh pot of coffee."

"Sounds great. Are you joining me today?"

The last few times I've been in, Mila has sat with me for several minutes, drinking her own cup of coffee and just talking. It's nice feeling like I have a friend in town; she introduced me to her brother the other day, Ethan, and their mutual friend Reid. Her brother is a big man, but seemed friendly enough. He's definitely not what I expected the mayor of this town to look like. Reid, the elementary school principal, gave off an easygoing vibe that makes total sense, seeing as it's summer break and he isn't dealing with hundreds of children every day. They're the kind of guys I wouldn't mind getting to know better, maybe have a beer with someday, but I'm in no hurry. Even though I feel like I'm settling in well enough, I still feel like my life has been in such chaos for the last few months I just need to take it slow.

"You bet I am." She heads into the back and comes out a moment later with a plate holding two scones, and a mug of coffee. Milo lumbers out after her, and heads straight to me, sitting beside me with his head on my lap.

"Hey, buddy," I say to the dog. "It's kind of awesome that he can be here with you all day."

Mila sits down across from me and smiles. "I know. Perks of a small town; no one cares."

"The sign in the window probably helps." I gesture over to the handwritten sign Mila put up that announces there is a dog inside. It was a smart choice to let anyone who might not like dogs know that Milo is inside. Although, from what I can gather, Mila hasn't had any issues. He's such a gentle dog, I'm not surprised that everyone loves him.

"Yeah, he does his rounds, greets everyone, then falls asleep on his bed for an hour around lunchtime. Rough life."

I can hear the affection in her voice. "He's lucky you found him."

She shakes her head. "Nope, I'm lucky he found me."

We share a smile. I won't deny, Mila is a beautiful woman. If my heart wasn't still recuperating from Stefani's betrayal, Mila is the kind of woman I'd be interested in. And for her to be as much of an animal lover as I am only makes her more attractive to me. But the best I can do is accept her friendship, and enjoy her company for now.

"Have you found a place to rent yet?"

I let out a quiet groan. "No. I understand that the rental market in a small town isn't exactly booming, but there's been absolutely nothing decent lately. I need more than a studio apartment, and the one house I found needed so much work. I don't have time for a renovation. I think I might have to look in Westport."

"Don't do that," Mila says, sitting up straight, a gleam coming into her eye. "Don't forget, you're looking at one of the Dogwood Cove land barons."

I laugh at that. "Oh, really. You think because you and your brother own some retail properties, you're at *land baron* status?"

"Ah, my naïve friend. You think all we own is retail? You'd be wrong. We've also got three rental houses. One of which is coming available in a few weeks when the Hillersons move to Vancouver."

It's my turn to sit up. "Are you serious?"

"Yup." She smiles triumphantly. "And since you've got an in with one of the landlords, I might be able to give you first dibs before we post the rental listing."

"God, Mila, that would be fucking amazing."

Mila gasps and brings her hand to her chest. "Why, Doctor Holt. I do believe that's the first time I've heard you curse. Is this town corrupting you?"

I burst into laughter at that. "Nobody is corrupting me, trust me. I guess we just haven't hung out enough for you to see the darker side of me."

Her light giggle fills the air. "Well it's nice to know you're not all bran muffins and starched shirts."

"Hey. I do not starch my shirts."

"Could have fooled me."

When I get to the clinic a little while later, I'm still smiling from my easy conversation with Mila. She's fun, lighthearted, and our banter today had me laughing more than I have in a long time. When I push open the doors to the clinic, Rosie, our receptionist, looks up at me with panic in her eyes.

"Doctor Holt, thank God. Doctor Morton is out at a foal delivery and I just got a call from Mrs. Wagner that her cat got hit by a car, and we've got a full slate of appointments today."

My eyes widen briefly. An emergency on top of a full caseload is not easy, especially since I'm here with just one technician. As much as I don't want to, I know what we need to do.

"Okay, Rosie. Call Veronica and see if she can come in to help out. Then send Doctor Morton a text, telling him *not* to rush back but letting him know what's happening. And let's go through the appointments for this morning and see who we can push to the afternoon. When is Mrs. Wagner going to be here?"

Fifteen minutes later, Rosie and I have cleared most of the morning except for some visits that a tech can handle, just as Mrs. Wagner walks in. Tears are streaming down her face and in her arms is a limp, furry body. My heart drops, but I push aside my emotions.

"Let me have Skip, and you sit down with Rosie to give her whatever information you can," I say gently. Veronica walks through the door, and I give her credit for how quickly she assesses the situation and joins the action.

"I'll wash up and meet you in the back, Doctor Holt."

I nod at her brusquely, already heading back with poor Skip. I can feel a faint heartbeat, but one leg is at an odd angle, and he's not very responsive. Still, I can tell how important this cat is to Mrs. Wagner, so I have to try and see what can be done.

For once, Veronica doesn't say or do anything inappropriate. We're all focused on helping Skip. Unfortunately, ultrasound reveals internal bleeding. Combined with his broken leg, and our limited capabilities for surgery, it means there's nothing we can do. I take a minute alone, stroking the now sedated cat's fur, trying to gather my composure before telling Mrs. Wagner that her best option is compassionate euthanasia. This is the hardest part of my job, and it never gets easier. Thankfully, although she is clearly devastated, Mrs. Wagner is able to agree that putting Skip down is what's best. I have our other technician, Martin, help me as he has been comforting Mrs. Wagner in between seeing other patients who we couldn't reschedule. Together we administer the medication to Skip, offer our condolences to Mrs. Wagner, then give her a moment by herself with her cat.

Out front, the waiting room is thankfully empty. Veronica and Rosie are standing behind the desk, waiting for us.

"Thank you all for your help this morning," I say quietly. Rosie has tears in her eyes, and we all stand there silently waiting for Mrs. Wagner. When she comes out, I hand her the packet we have prepared for this situation, we all say our condolences and goodbyes. But there's no time to dwell on the sadness, because our next patient arrives and it's time to try and catch up from our morning.

I end up staying at the clinic long after it closes, finishing case notes and other tasks that I simply didn't have time for earlier. When I'm done, the last thing I want to do is go back to an empty motel room. It's too late to hit the water and go for a paddle, but Martin mentioned he and his partner, who happens to work at Mila's bakery, would be going out to Hastings, the local bar in town, and invited me along.

So, after stopping at the motel to shower, change, and spend some time with Harley — which feels extra poignant after what happened today — I head out on foot to the bar. When I walk inside, my gaze sweeps the room, looking for Martin and Sebastian. I find them easily enough, and when I see Mila sitting with them, my mood picks up instantly.

"Jackson, hey!" It's clear she wasn't expecting me tonight, but I think she's happy to see me.

"Hi. I didn't realize you would be here, too," I reply, settling down into an empty chair beside her.

She slides over a pitcher of beer and an empty glass. "Yeah, well, I don't have to open the bakery tomorrow, which means I can stay up past nine tonight." She wiggles her fingers in mock excitement, and I chuckle.

"Living the good life." It feels natural to tease her, and her laugh eases some of the darkness that had settled in my heart after the day we had. When she leans over and squeezes my arm, I look into her deep brown eyes.

"Martin filled us in on your day. Poor Skip, I'm going to drop off some muffins for Mrs. Wagner tomorrow. Are you okay?"

Her words touch me, and I'm surprised to realize it's the first time in my career that anyone has bothered to ask me how I am after euthanizing a pet. That shouldn't be true, but it is. Stefani claimed she "couldn't bear to think about it," and I was always the one ensuring other staff were alright.

"I'm okay. It's always sad, but it's part of the job."

Mila looks at me closely for a moment but whatever she sees in my face seems to satisfy her.

"Alright. Then let's drink some beer, shoot some pool, and have a good night."

We cheers our glasses of beer together and drink. As the cold beer slides down my throat, I feel the stress of the day start to leave. Whether it's the drink or the company, I don't fucking care right now.

"You must be the new vet." A woman's voice comes at me from across the table. When I look up I see that it belongs to someone who is vaguely familiar, but I'm sure we haven't met. "I'm Serena, one of Mila's best friends."

I reach my hand over the table to shake hers. "Jackson, nice to meet you. And yes, I'm the new vet."

"Cool. Welcome to town," she replies. I give her a nod of thanks and take another sip of my beer, letting the conversations around me happen without really taking part in any of it. Don't get me wrong, it feels good to be out with some other people my age, hopefully making connections and friends, but I can also feel the emotional weight of not just today, but the last several months threatening to overtake me.

"Hi, Jackson."

Shit. A hand lands on my shoulder at the same time I hear Veronica's voice, which sounds way too close to my ear. I didn't even notice her, much less realize she had gotten so close. I shift my chair ever so slightly toward Mila, who's on my other side, but Veronica doesn't back away.

"Hi, Veronica. How are you?" I keep my tone polite, but hopefully not exactly inviting to conversation. It's a fine balance of maintaining respect for my co-worker, and not opening the door to any more problems.

"I'm okay; in need of some...comfort. It's okay for me to call you Jackson, right? Since we aren't at work and all..." She bats her eyelashes at me, and I stifle a groan. Seriously, does she think this approach works? It's way too blatant for me.

"I hope you've got some friends you're meeting." My mind is whirring, trying to figure out how the hell to get out of this, when someone calls her name from across the bar. Thank fuck. She frowns at them, and for an instant I'm worried she'll ignore them. But she doesn't.

"I'll see you tomorrow," she says, the words laced with an uncomfortable innuendo, and her hand squeezes my shoulder before she walks away. A small sigh of relief escapes me, and Mila hears it.

"I see she's got her claws in you," she says with a giggle. I arch my brow at her as I drink my beer.

"Yeah, you could say that."

"She's relentless, just so you know. Nothing short of a two by four will get through her thick skull when she wants something." Mila's blunt assessment of how dogged Veronica seems to be about pursuing me makes me chuckle.

"I shouldn't laugh. She's my colleague. But it's getting pretty awkward."

"So you're not interested in fake boobs and spider eye lashes?" Mila blinks her own eyes rapidly, and I can't help but notice how pretty hers are.

"Definitely not. I prefer a more natural woman," I reply honestly. Something's shifting between us, and I don't think

I'm ready for it. Before I can think about what I'm saying, I continue. "Besides, I have zero interest in dating right now. I'm here to get my career established, join Doctor Morton as partner, and then I'll figure out the rest of my life."

Mila lifts her own glass. "Amen to no time for dating. I'm way too focused on figuring out if I can expand the bakery. Besides, no man wants to put up with my insane hours."

She takes a long drink of beer, and I wonder if there's something behind her words. They sounded almost vulnerable. We're both quiet for a minute, then Serena walks over with a pool cue.

"Come on you two, we need a second pair to play."

Mila stands up, glass in hand, and looks down at me. "What do you say, winner buys the next round?"

I stand up as well and refill my glass before responding. In my head I debate whether I should tell her how many nights I spent playing pool in between studying for exams in university.

"You're on."

# Chapter Five

*Mila*

Seeing Jackson at Hastings last week was a welcome surprise. The man that I initially thought was aloof and stuck up is gone, and the Jackson I'm getting to know now is funny, charming, and a really good pool player. I still smile when I remember how duped I was that night when he absolutely dominated our game. Don't get me wrong, watching my friend Reid get taken down a notch was amazing; he's been the winner more often than not, until last week, that is. But what I was totally unprepared for was how sexy Jackson looked, stretching out to line up his shot, his muscles straining against the confines of his shirt. Obviously, I can say he is an attractive guy, I drooled over his forearms the first day I saw him. But something was different seeing him in a casual environment. He was far too tempting, and I was damn glad my friends were around to stop me from doing anything stupid.

The Dogwood Cove Summer Solstice Festival came just a couple of days after our evening at Hastings, and I found myself searching the crowd for Jackson, wondering if he was enjoying the festival, but I didn't see him there.

Early summer on the west coast of Canada is my absolute favourite time of year. It's warming up, but isn't yet super hot. The sun shines more often than not, and the days are getting long. The sunrise when I get to the bakery is spectacular almost every single morning, and there's just something about late spring that makes me feel hopeful for the future.

With the longer days, I'm spending most of my limited spare time outside. When I pull up to the public beach one afternoon with Milo, my head is preoccupied with a conversation my brother and I had earlier this week. Ethan and I figured out that I can finally start the expansion into the space next to the bakery and open the café Mom and I had always planned. So all I can think about these days is what I want to add to the menu to include more lunch items — soups, quiches, sandwiches, that kind of thing. And last night, while I was sitting on my back porch watching Milo play, and drinking a local beer, I started thinking about pretzels. Soft pretzels would be easy to make; a good snack item to have on hand at the bakery and something that Summer could even sell at the resort when she opens later this summer.

I guess my friends are right that I'm a total workaholic, because all I can think about is the bakery. Even on my days off. In fact, I'm so wrapped up in pretzel dipping sauce ideas that I don't notice anyone is at the beach until I hear my name. Milo starts to bark, and pull on his leash, and I look up only to trip over my own feet.

If I thought Jackson was attractive in a T-shirt and jeans, that's nothing compared to what he looks like shirtless, wearing low slung board shorts and bare feet. His hair isn't styled, and the breeze is making it blow around his face. He's got a wide, relaxed grin on his face, and a paddle board at his feet.

"Are you following me, Miss Monroe?" His eyes are alight with friendly teasing.

"I don't know about that, after all, you're the one who comes into my bakery every morning. Maybe you're following me." I unclip Milo's leash and he goes straight over to Jackson, who bends down to give him some affection.

"His leg doesn't seem to be bothering him as much," he comments, running his hands down Milo's legs.

"Hey, you're not on duty, Doctor Holt."

He grins up at me, and my breath catches. Seeing him like this — happy, casual, *and did I mention shirtless*— is making my heartbeat go haywire.

"Can't help it. Are you here so he can swim?"

I nod. It's something he had mentioned to me at the bakery one morning as a way to help Milo exercise without irritating his leg. "Yeah, he seems to really enjoy it. Especially if we find a good stick." I drop my eyes down to the ground under the pretense of looking for a stick. The reality is I need to stop looking at Jackson's chest. I spy a good one, and walk over to grab it, then head down to the water's edge. Milo follows, and I throw it as far as I can, watching him splash through the shallows carefully until it gets deep enough for him to swim. It must feel good, because he doesn't come back right away, choosing instead to get the stick and then swim around for a minute or two.

"He looks good out there." Jackson comes up beside me, and I'm relieved to see he's put on a shirt.

"He seems to love swimming. Thanks for suggesting it," I reply, sitting down on a log. Jackson settles down beside me, and we both watch Milo swim for a while longer. When he comes out with his stick, he goes to Jackson, not me, which should feel strange since he's my dog, but I find I don't mind. Watching a sexy man play with a dog is hot as hell. Jackson throws the stick out in the water, and off goes Milo again.

"You missed the festival this weekend," I comment.

"Yeah, believe it or not, we had a lot of appointments that day. I heard it was pretty good. What goes on at it?"

"It's the usual — carnival games, food vendors, a few rides for the kids. But Ethan was somehow able to get Nash Parker to play for the concert and didn't tell anyone. That was cool." We fall silent for a few minutes, watching Milo swim and play in the water. "I've been wondering, what brought you to Dogwood Cove?" I ask after a while. "Small towns aren't normally a draw for single people."

He gives me a questioning look in return. "Do you always say whatever you're thinking?"

"Pretty much." I lift my shoulders and give him a wry grin. "Why bother dancing around a subject when I'm curious."

"Fair enough." Jackson leans back on the log, putting his hands on either side of his hips. That brings his shoulder close enough to me to brush against my arm, and I can feel the heat radiating from him. "Two things brought me here. The opportunity to eventually partner with Doctor Morton and be my own boss, and a need to get away from some shit that happened in my life."

"What kind of shit? Are we talking jilted ex, or running from the law, or witness protection plan?"

His loud laugh booms across the beach, startling some nearby seagulls. Milo comes back with his stick, and Jackson throws it again before answering.

"Close, but no." He dusts his hands off, and looks at me, his expression suddenly serious. "You really want to know?"

I nod.

"My fiancée revealed to me that she had been lying for years about not wanting a family. As in she wanted kids despite telling me she didn't. I had made it clear right from the beginning that children were not something I wanted, and she pretended to agree. We were two months out from our wedding when she finally admitted the truth. Turns out she had hoped to change my mind, or trick me, who knows. But when she finally realized I was serious, she decided to come clean. I guess it's better that she did it before the wedding and not after, but it hurt. Then I found out my boss at the animal shelter I was working at had been caught embezzling funds. The entire organization was bankrupt and going under. As soon as we found new shelter spaces for the animals, I quit. Took a couple weeks to get drunk and be miserable, then started looking for a job. The posting here seemed almost too good to be true, but when I spoke with Doctor Morton and came over for an interview, it seemed like the perfect way to start over. And here I am. Living in a motel with my cat, working with a woman who doesn't seem to take no for an answer, but happier than I have been in a long time. I can see my future, and it's looking good."

When he stops talking, we sit in silence for a moment. That's a lot he's just revealed to me, and truthfully, I'm not sure what to say in response. Milo interrupts the moment by coming up to us and shaking salt water everywhere before collapsing down in the sand.

"I guess he's done for the day," Jackson says conversationally, as if he hasn't just shared his deepest, darkest secrets.

"Thank you for telling me all that," I blurt out. "I mean, I know you didn't have to, we don't know each other that well, so thank you for trusting me with it."

When I glance over at him, he's looking at me with an odd expression on his face. "Mila, we're friends. At least, in my mind we are. I didn't tell you any of that to burden you with it, or to get sympathy. You asked why I'm here, and that's the answer. It's not a secret, it just is what it is."

I nod slowly, then reach over and squeeze his hand. "For what it's worth, your ex is a bitch for lying to you."

"Thanks." He huffs out a low laugh that's full of pain. "I thought I had hit the jackpot, finding a woman who had similar goals and wants to mine. When I told her I didn't want to have children, she didn't even blink, just agreed with me. To find out she was lying the whole time, hoping to persuade me to change my mind once we were married, it felt like she ripped the ground out from right under my feet."

I'm nervous to say what I know I need to say. But Jackson has been so open and honest with me, I want to do the same. "It's weird for women. We're programmed from birth to believe we should want to have kids. Be a wife and a mother, that's our role. And for most women, that's fine, that's what they want. But when you don't...it's hard to convince people you're not crazy."

Jackson looks at me with surprise and doubt written all over his face. It doesn't bother me, after what he's been through; I don't expect him to believe me right away. "You don't want kids?"

I shake my head slowly. "Nope. My bakery is my baby. Growing up I didn't play with dolls, I played with toy kitchens and made mud pies. I knew I wanted to bake and feed people. Sure, I'd love to get married, and don't get me wrong, kids are fun to be around, but I want to be able to hand them back to their mom or dad when they start to cry or take a dump."

Jackson snorts softly, and his eyes are still searching my face, looking for the truth that I hope is written plainly there.

"Honestly, I would love it if Ethan and Summer had kids someday. I think I'd be an amazing auntie. But I have zero intention of having my own children. Society can just fuck off if they want to tell me otherwise."

"It shouldn't be considered a crime to want something different than what other people want."

He speaks so low, and the words are filled with so much anger and sadness, it's a struggle to not reach out and offer him some physical comfort. But we aren't there yet in our relationship, or friendship, whatever this is between us. He's my dog's vet, and a new friend. Nothing more. Neither one of us want it to be anything more. Instead, I stand up and Milo climbs to his feet with me. When I look back down at Jackson, he seems lost in thought, staring out at the ocean.

"I think standing up for what you want in life is the bravest thing anyone can do. Especially when someone tries to convince you that you're wrong." I pause, trying to figure out the right thing to say. "But you are not wrong, Jackson. She was wrong for lying to you, for not respecting how you feel. I'm glad you came here for a fresh start. Maybe Dogwood Cove is the right place for a single guy after all."

Jackson snaps out of whatever moment he was having and stands up. But the smile he gives me doesn't reach all the way to his eyes, and I can sense him pulling back, putting some distance between us and the emotionally heavy conversation we've just had.

"It's definitely the right place for this single guy." He brushes some sand off his leg, then straightens up. "Speaking of the right place, any chance you can show me that house that I might be able to rent?"

I take the change in subject without saying anything. "Sure. The current renters will be out midweek, then Ethan wants to get in there and do any repairs that are needed and give it a fresh coat of paint. So as long as you don't mind viewing it while he's there working, we can go by any afternoon next week."

"Sounds like a plan, thanks." He lets out a sigh of relief. "This'll hopefully get Morton to back off a bit, too."

"What do you mean?"

He let's out a small groan, and I'd be lying if my head didn't wonder what that groan would sound like under more...intimate circumstances.

"He's made it clear that partnership is contingent upon me being *settled* in Dogwood Cove. I don't think he likes the fact that I'm single, and he definitely doesn't like that I'm living in a motel."

"What, he wants you married with two point five children before he offers you the job?" I laugh at how ridiculous it sounds, but instantly sober when I see Jackson nodding his head with a slight grimace. "Wait. Seriously?"

"Yeah, it seems that way. He hasn't outright said it, but he's definitely said he's waiting to see if I'm committed to the town."

"What is with people thinking everyone needs to be in a relationship to be happy? Why can't we just be happy by ourselves?" I don't realize how frustrated I sound until I catch Jackson's look of surprise.

"Everything okay?"

I let out a long sigh. "Yeah, just an over involved brother and best friend who think it's wrong I'm not happy and in love like they are. Apparently I work too much and have no life. They don't understand that I have goals and dreams, and a relationship would only get in the way of that right now."

"Damn."

I nod, and we turn to walk back to our cars. When we reach them, I realize I don't exactly want to say goodbye. It's been fun spending this time with him instead of by myself.

"Thanks for, you know, listening today." Jackson rubs his hand over his chin. "It felt good to talk about everything."

A smile creeps across my face, because he's right. It did feel good. "Same for me. I guess I'll see you tomorrow?" I'm weirdly nervous for his reply. Like I need to know that our confessions today didn't screw up the friendship we've started.

"That depends. What are you baking?" His tone is teasing, and I instantly relax.

"Carrot muffins." Talking about food is always a good way to ease any tension for me.

"How is a carrot muffin any better than a bran muffin?" He actually sounds offended, and it makes me laugh.

"Easy. Carrot cake is delicious. Have you ever heard of *bran cake*?" I shudder.

"But you're not making cake, you're making muffins,"

"Which are mini cakes, only slightly healthier," I state matter-of-factly. Now we're both chuckling, and any nerves I had are gone. "Try a carrot muffin tomorrow, and if you can honestly tell me they aren't amazing, I'll give you free bran muffins for a month."

"You need to stop making deals with me, didn't our game of pool teach you anything?" he teases, his eyes dancing with mischief.

"Sure. It taught me never to bet against you in pool. But unless you have a secret past as a baker, I'm pretty sure I can win this one."

He holds his hands up in mock surrender. "You're probably right. Okay, see you tomorrow morning for a *carrot* muffin."

"It's going to change your world," I say in a somber voice.

Jackson chuckles as he climbs into his car. "Can't wait."

Interestingly enough, neither can I.

# Chapter Six

*Jackson*

I'm not going to admit that I keep checking for Mila in the waiting room every time I escort a patient out to the front after their appointment, because that would mean admitting that I like her.

And I do like her.

Probably more than I should right now.

Which is why I'm also not admitting that the carrot muffin she made me eat this morning was by far one of the best muffins I've ever had in my life. And I love muffins.

She said this morning that she would stop by the clinic after work with something for me, so when the clock strikes four and I haven't seen her yet, I start to think maybe she was in and out while I was with a patient. But why would she come here and not wait to see me?

Fuck. I'm overthinking this more than the Nashville Fury overthink their offensive plays.

"Hey, Doctor Holt. You look like you could use a massage, your muscles are so tense. You should come over tonight to relax, I'll order some dinner and I've got a bottle of red at home with our name on it."

It's probably not a good thing that when I hear Veronica's voice all I feel is dread. And when that voice is dangerously close by, my gut reaction is to move as far away as I politely can. Unfortunately, I'm trapped between the side of the counter and Veronica, who's pressing into me in a way that is completely inappropriate for the workplace. This is my punishment for being so pathetic that I'm hanging out by the front desk hoping to see Mila, instead of being in the back, finishing up chart notes so I can leave for the day.

"Hey, honey," Mila's sweet voice is a godsend, and it takes me a second to register the fact that she is calling someone honey. And in that second, my confusion goes from level one to level ten when she walks straight up to me, neatly shoving Veronica to the side. She puts her hand on my chest, lifts up onto her toes, and kisses me lightly on the lips. It's brief enough my brain doesn't even have time to register the sensation of someone other than Stefani kissing me for the first time in years. But other parts of my body definitely seem to take notice.

I'm trying to catch up, completely confused by what just happened, and have no idea how to respond until Mila keeps talking.

"I'm glad I got to see you. I wasn't sure how busy you would be; I know you want to get out in time for dinner at my place."

Mila's fluttering her eyelashes at me, but when I look closer, I see mischief in her brown eyes. Then it clicks. She's giving me an out with Veronica. This is going to be awkward as all hell later, but for now I'll take the excuse she's offering.

"Hi, babe. Can't wait, I'm almost done here." I lean down and kiss her again on instinct, and I'm surprised that it feels as good as it does to have her lips against mine. They're soft, and they fit against mine in a way that is eerily perfect. I take a step back to put some space between us. Yeah, she's a beautiful woman and I'm a guy who isn't afraid to admit that, but she's also a friend. A friend who is just helping me with a sticky situation. At least, I think that's what she's doing.

Whatever game Mila's playing works, because Veronica steps even further away, and is watching us with a glower on her face and her hands crossed in front of her chest.

"What are *you* doing here?" she asks, and holy shit, the tone of her voice is cold enough to freeze water. Something tells me there's history between these two, and it isn't friendly.

"Not that it's any of your business, but *Jackson*," I smirk at how Mila emphasizes my first name, "has been helping me with Milo's leg. I'm here to get some more medicine for him and bring some more thank you cookies for *my man*." Sure enough Mila hands me a bag that smells of chocolate. This must be the real reason she's here.

Oh God. It's so cheesy, and I'm thankful the only person witnessing this is Rosie, who is manning the front desk again today. She's watching us raptly, and I swear if there was popcorn in front of her, she'd be eating it. Little did I know when I came to work today that I'd be putting on a show. Meanwhile, Veronica looks like she could spit fire at Mila, and a part of me worries if I'll be breaking up a fight in a minute.

"Anyway, I'll see you at my house later, honey." Mila presses one more kiss, this time to my jaw, before walking over to the door. As she goes, my eyes are drawn to her hips, which sway back and forth with each step. It's all part of the show she's putting on for Veronica, but that doesn't mean I can't appreciate the sight.

When I turn back to Veronica and Rosie, they're both staring at me. One with frustration and defeat in her eyes, and one with excitement.

"Alright then. Back to work," I say brusquely, then I push through the doors and go straight to the back office to bury myself in paperwork until my next patient. And to try and make sense of what just happened. More importantly, how I'm going to handle the fact that kissing Mila Monroe felt really, really good.

I finish up my work for the day just before six. I haven't heard from Mila, but I also haven't had to deal with any more advances from Veronica, which is a relief. The number of times I picked up my phone to text Mila is embarrassing, especially since I don't know what I would say.

*Thanks for helping me with Veronica.*

*Your lips feel amazing.*

*I want to kiss you again.*

Yeah, no. Not going there.

When I leave the clinic, my stomach is growling, but I don't want to go out anywhere to eat. A pre-made meal from the grocery store is all I need for now. And a drink. I definitely need a drink. Thank God this grocery store is one that can sell alcohol. The choices are limited to local BC wines, but there are some excellent choices.

I walk up to the cashier with my basket, and when I unload the bottle of wine I picked out, she gives me a knowing smile. "Taking this over to Mila Monroe's house?" she says with a wink.

"Uh, yeah. That's right," I say awkwardly. What the hell? Why is a complete stranger at the store asking if I'm going to Mila's? For that matter, why did I say yes?

Back at the motel I drink wine out of my coffee cup while Harley purrs on my lap. He really is the laziest cat ever, but we've been together for years. I mull over what went on at the clinic today. As far as a strategy to get Veronica off my back, it worked, but what happens now? Eventually I go to bed, hoping that things will be more clear tomorrow.

Oh, how wrong I was. The next morning, thanks to a lovely red wine hangover, I sleep in late. Which means I don't have time to stop by the bakery and talk to Mila before going to the clinic. In fact, by the time I get up and ready, all I have time for is a quick protein shake as I drive to work. I'll have to make do with the nasty coffee in the break room at the clinic today, even though my taste buds are whimpering at not getting something to eat from The Nutty Muffin.

Needless to say, I'm completely off my game, which also means I'm completely unprepared for the reception that awaits me when I walk into the office and see Doctor Morton there.

"Jackson, my boy, wonderful to see you. I can't tell you how happy I am to hear you're finding your way here in our town."

That's a strange comment to make, but I roll with it. "Ah, thanks, Phil. I'm really enjoying it here. In fact, I'll be looking at a house with Mila Monroe this weekend —"

"Looking at houses together? Well now, you seem to be moving quickly, but what do I know. Young love." he interrupts me, standing up and coming over to put his hands on my shoulder. I'm frozen in shock, trying to understand what the hell is happening. "I'm happy for you. Sharon and I will have to have the two of you over for dinner sometime soon. It'll be a great opportunity to chat more about your future here."

He walks out of the office, whistling, and I'm left standing there, my heart pounding in my ears. Why the hell does Doctor Morton think I'm in love with Mila Monroe?

I open my phone and finally send a message to Mila.

**JACKSON: We need to talk.**

**MILA: Yeah, we do. Rosie spilled the beans about yesterday.**

**JACKSON: Rosie?**

**MILA: Yep. She's the biggest gossip in town. She probably texted her knitting club, which is the fastest way for news to spread like wildfire. Sorry, I should've thought of that before I...you know.**

**JACKSON: Before you kissed me.**

**MILA: Yeah. That. Look, just come by my place tonight after work. I have an idea.**

I pocket my phone and take a deep breath. Whatever is going on, it's a simple misunderstanding. We just need to explain it to...everyone? Fuck. Does the whole damn town think I'm dating Mila? I internally groan thinking about Phil's reaction when I tell him it's all a mistake. This isn't going to bode well for my partnership.

I head out to the waiting room, where thankfully, Rosie is *not* working, so I don't have to pretend I'm not mad at her for spreading lies. Although I guess she didn't know she was spreading lies. All I have to do is get through the next nine hours, then I can go to Mila's and we can figure out how to get out of this mess.

By the time I get to Mila's house I'm grumpy and exhausted from having to deal with patient after patient who had something to say about my "relationship" with Mila.

Every goddamn time I wanted to tell them *there is no relationship,* but I stopped myself. I need to talk to her, and get our story straight before I try and fight down the tidal wave of rumours I was flooded with. Everything from Mila being the real reason I moved to Dogwood Cove, to us moving in together, to her being pregnant. That last one I *did* shut down pretty damn fast.

Apparently, no one knows gossip like a small town.

When I walk up to her door, I'm struck by a few things. First of all, her house is perfect for her. It's small and cute, with well kept gardens out front and a stone path leading up to the front door. Part of me wonders how the hell she has time to garden, since it seems she's always at the bakery, but Mila strikes me as an overachiever in the best sense of the word. The next thing I notice is the door mat that reads "If you're pizza, Amazon, or Ryan Gosling, I'M HOME". That brings a real smile to my face for the first time all day, and I wish I had thought to bring something for dinner. Pizza sounds amazing right now.

Before I can even knock on the door, I hear Milo's deep bark from inside, and Mila's voice telling him he's a good boy. I respect the fact she isn't trying to stop his natural instinct to notify her of someone on the property, especially since she lives alone.

"Hi, come in, don't let the scary beast get you," she says as she opens the door. Milo sneaks past her and prances around at my feet until I crouch down and give him some attention. Then I stand up, and we head inside. The interior of her house matches her personality perfectly. It's bright and colourful, with photos of her and Ethan, and of her and her friends everywhere.

"Are you hungry?" she asks as she heads into what I assume is the kitchen. I follow, Milo by my side.

"Starved, actually. But you don't have to feed me, we could order pizza; your door mat tells me that would be a good idea." I give her another smile. What is it about this woman that makes me smile all the damn time?

She puts her hands on her hips and looks at me, bringing her lip between her teeth. "You're no Ryan Gosling, but if you're offering pizza, you can stay."

I chuckle, and just like that, all of my stress from the crazy day I've had fades away. The only other thing that gets me to relax that easily is being on the ocean, or sex.

But I'm not going there.

"So, today was interesting," I say after the pizza is ordered and we're settled on her couch with a beer in hand.

"Oh my God, right?" she moans, flopping her head back. "I swear, *every single person* that came in today had something to say about our new relationship. I knew gossip travels fast, but damn."

"I had someone ask if I got you pregnant."

She bolts upright and looks at me in horror. "No. Way."

I nod and take a pull from my beer. "Don't worry, I corrected them. No one needs to know about our secret love child until we're ready."

Unfortunately, just as I say that Mila is mid-swallow, so she starts to choke with laughter.

"Shit, sorry, are you okay?" I put my beer down and lean over, but the second my hand touches her bare shoulder I pull it away. I don't know if I should touch her right now.

"I'm fine. Just, shit. Didn't realize you had that in you."

"What, a sense of humour?"

"No. Well, yes. I mean, ah fuck." She drops back against the couch again and lifts her arm up to cover her face. "I'd say I'm sorry for what I did yesterday, but it looked like Veronica was two seconds away from stripping naked and jumping you right there in the clinic."

I grimace at the memory. "You're not far off. She offered me a massage."

"*What?*"

I nod. "Seriously. She said something about me looking tense, and how she had a bottle of wine at home for us. It might have made things complicated, but your little lie saved my ass from one hell of an awkward situation."

Mila drops her gaze to her beer bottle and starts to pick at the label. "Here's the thing. What if it wasn't a lie?"

I'm stunned into silence. And confusion. When I find my voice, I choose my words carefully. The last thing I want to do is hurt her. "Mila, you're awesome, don't get me wrong. Any guy would be lucky to date you. But..."

"Oh God, no!" She puts her hand out and shakes her head emphatically. "No. Jackson, I'm not saying we should be to-gether. No. I don't have time to date, and you don't want to date. We're friends, and that's perfectly fine, and more than enough for me."

"Thank fuck," I breathe, and we both laugh quietly. "So, what are you saying?"

"Hear me out," she says, turning her body to face me. "What if we fake date?"

I raise my eyebrow at that. "Fake date?"

"Yeah. We go out together, hold hands, let everyone think we're together. But it's all for show. Then after a few months, when my family is off my back about my nonexistent love life, and you've got your partnership, we realize we're better as friends and go our separate ways. Easy peasy lemon squeezy."

"I'm going to have to pretend you didn't just say easy peasy lemon squeezy," I say drily as my brain spins, trying to make sense of her suggestion. It's smart and crazy. But especially smart. "So, you're saying we go out together as friends, but let people think we're more than that."

She nods. "Exactly. I'll help you convince Morton that you're settled in Dogwood Cove, and you'll help me convince my friends that I'm not doomed to be a workaholic spinster my entire life."

Spending time with Mila isn't exactly a hardship. And I can think of a million ways this could go wrong. But she's got a point. Being in a relationship, especially with someone like Mila who is such an important part of this town, would probably go a long way to convincing Morton that I'm here to stay. If we keep clear boundaries, and don't lose sight of why we're only pretending, maybe this could work. I'll just have to remind myself that she's faking it when she kisses me. Even if it feels pretty damn real.

"You're on."

# Chapter Seven

*Mila*

Fake dating Jackson is either the best idea I've ever had or the worst. Only time will tell which one it turns out to be. I have to admit, I wasn't thinking clearly when I kissed him at the clinic; I just saw Veronica with her bitchy talons in him, and the look of pure discomfort on his face, and I acted.

But that kiss.

That kiss took me by surprise. I didn't expect to enjoy it that much, or want to do it again right away. I certainly didn't expect the zing I felt run up and down my spine when our lips touched. But oh man, did I ever zing.

We've made plans for our first fake date to be tomorrow night. I'm hoping that the town's insane interest in my dating life will die down soon, because I swear if I have one more customer ask me some outrageous question about Jackson and I, I might scream. Granted, it didn't help that when he walked into the bakery this morning, he came around the end of the counter and kissed the top of my head before pouring his coffee.

You could hear the collective swoon of everyone in the place. Okay, it was pretty sweet. I guess I'm just not used to this kind of attention. It makes my skin itch. It reminds me too much of the way the town was after my parents died. Well intentioned, full of love, but goddamn, everyone would just *not* leave me and Ethan alone.

Yeah, I definitely did not anticipate the reaction of everyone in town, but that was my mistake. I remember when Lisa and Kenny Barker started dating, and it was all the town could talk about for a week. Somehow Ethan and Summer dodged the gossip train earlier this spring, but I guess Jackson and I aren't so lucky.

"What did that bread dough do to you?"

My friend Paige's voice pierces through my fog as I'm in the middle of kneading dough.

"What?" I say, completely confused. Looking down at the dough, I realize it does look a little overworked. I guess I wasn't paying attention.

"I brought you a copy of the questions for tonight, just in case you haven't had a chance to review them yet."

I'm still staring at her blankly. Not only did I not hear her come into the kitchen, but I have no idea what she's talking about.

"Book club. It's tonight. I do hope you've finished the book. Our conversation should be interesting, as Serena has already informed me that she is not a fan of the secret baby trope."

Finally, my damn brain catches up with what she's saying. "Right. Book club. Tonight."

Paige sits down on a stool and sets the piece of paper she's holding down on the counter. Then she peers at me through her glasses. "You forgot, didn't you?"

I wince. "Sorry. I guess I've just been so distracted with everything."

"You mean like the new vet? There certainly is a lot of gossip around town about you two."

I nod slowly. "Yeah. That."

Paige taps the paper. "Review the questions. And be prepared for questions about *you* as well. Serena is not happy that she had to hear about you and Doctor Holt from Annabelle at the grocery store."

Ah crap. "Yeah, sorry. It's...new. I was going to tell you guys soon, I promise."

"You'll have a chance to fill us in tonight. Bring cookies."

Always one to get straight to the point, Paige stands up, picks up a scone from where they're cooling on the counter, and waves as she leaves, heading next door to her bookstore.

Dammit. I completely forgot tonight is book club night. That means I need to figure out what I'm going to say to my friends about Jackson and I, and fast. Those girls are nosy and Paige is particularly perceptive.

And I am not a good liar.

This should be interesting.

We're meeting at Paige's house again tonight, and she's not as big a fan of dogs as Summer and I are. Which means I don't have Milo by my side as I walk the two blocks over to her house with a bottle of wine in one hand and a container of cookies in the other.

When I push open the front door, the conversation inside stops. Apparently, I'm the last one to arrive out of the four of us, and I'm *also* the center of all of their attention.

"I *knew* it!" Serena cries out, leaping to her feet and dancing across the room to take the wine from my hand. "I knew you two had something going on when I saw you at the bar the other night." She pirouettes on her feet as she heads for the kitchen and glares at me. "You know, you could have told me."

I ignore the looks Paige and Summer are giving me and follow Serena, mostly for the wine. "What are you talking about? We weren't together at the bar." That, at least, is the truth. "We, umm, started dating after." God, this is awful. I hate lying.

"Seriously? Well, it was inevitable then. The way he was looking at you? Oh man, I thought I would get electrocuted from the sparks flying. And I saw you mooning over him."

"Mooning? I do not moon."

"There was that one time in kindergarten," Summer pipes up with a mischievous smile.

"Oh my God, we were five." I say, my voice laden with exasperation. "Is tonight just going to be *tease Mila* night? Because I'll take my wine and leave if it is."

Summer and Serena crowd me in the kitchen, wrapping their arms around me while Paige walks past us to take something out of the oven.

"Sorry, Mila. We're just excited for you," Summer says gently.

"And pissed you didn't tell us. Not that I blame you, he is one sexy vet."

"Serena. Not helping," Summer chides.

I disentangle myself from their arms and go back to pouring a healthy glass of wine. "I get it guys, I should have told you. But it's new, and kinda weird because he's Milo's vet."

Paige sets down a platter with some sort of appetizer on it. I don't even care that they're store bought, I'm just grateful to have something to hopefully distract everyone from the interrogation. I should have known better, not even food will get these girls to lose focus. I pick one up and take a small bite. Serena grabs one and shoves the whole thing in her mouth before fixing me with a stare.

"Mmmduninkma'er."

"What the hell did you just say?" I ask, watching as crumbs fall out of her mouth. For a dance teacher who is meant to personify elegance and grace, she is a hot mess sometimes.

She swallows and takes a sip of wine before replying. "I said, I don't think that matters. It's not like human doctors and patients, where there's a power imbalance. He's your dog's doctor, not yours. You're fine."

Paige lifts her glass of wine and a small plate with some food on it, and gestures to the living room.

"Agreed. There is no impropriety in the two of you pursuing a relationship. Now, shall we move to the living room and begin our discussion of this month's book?"

I send a silent prayer of thanks to Paige and her ridiculous organization skills. This might only be our third book club meeting, but it's very clear that she takes it seriously. Much more seriously than the rest of us do, that's for sure.

Sure enough, for the next hour she keeps us on task, debating the merits of the book we read. Honestly, I barely remember it. Since finding Milo on the side of the road just a few weeks ago, I feel like my life has been one crazy thing after another. But I manage to hold my own in the conversation, which naturally turns to a debate over which sex scene was the hottest. My reprieve doesn't last forever, though. When we've gone through all of Paige's questions — a first, I might add— Summer refills our wine glasses and all eyes turn back to me.

"Okay. Now that we've all agreed keeping a pregnancy secret from the father is not a story line any of us enjoy, can we *please* talk about the romance unfolding in real life?" Serena turns to me and rubs her hands together gleefully. "I want all the dirty deets. Is he a good kisser? Have you slept with him? Does he like doggy style?" She snorts after her last question and I raise my eyebrow.

"How much wine have you had?"

She's still giggling to herself, so Paige answers. "She's finished almost one bottle."

"It's the dance moms. I swear they're going to drive me to an early grave," Serena moans. "Nina needs a private lesson. Taryn should be given a solo. Why didn't you spend any time with Farrah," she says in a mocking tone. "Seriously, they all think their little butterfly is the most precious thing ever, but what they don't get is, I have a class *full* of girls who all deserve attention and private lessons and solos. But I can't give it to them all."

I cringe, because it does sound pretty annoying trying to deal with demanding dance moms. But I keep quiet, because magically, Serena has managed to switch the conversation away from her annoying questions about Jackson and I onto herself. I hate lying, and lying to my best friends is even worse. I might need to talk to Jackson about letting the girls in on our plan, because I don't know if I can keep this up, and we haven't even gone on our first "date." Not to mention, if the whole point was to get everyone off my back about my love life, then this is already an epic failure. If anything, the attention and the questions have become worse.

By the time seven o'clock rolls around the next evening, I am mentally and physically exhausted. Not only was it another long day at the bakery, but I'm still fielding comments and questions about my new relationship. At this point, all I can hope is that something else happens in town for everyone to focus on, but that's the curse of a small town. Your business is everyone's business until something new and exciting happens.

Something tells me that tonight is only going to fuel the fire of everyone gossiping about us. It will be our first time out in public pretending to be together. We're keeping it simple, with dinner at Bella Mia, the one fancy-ish restaurant in town. It's cheesy and predictable. But our options are limited if we want to maximize exposure. Going to Westport for dinner doesn't really achieve our goal of solidifying our status as a couple.

A knock at the door sends Milo into his usual barking frenzy. When I open the door, my stupid heart flutters. Jackson in a dress shirt with the sleeves rolled up is sexy. Jackson shirtless on the beach is sexy.

Jackson wearing a leather jacket over a fitted black V-neck shirt and dark jeans is...something beyond sexy.

"You look beautiful." His voice rumbles over me, sending chills down my spine. The good kind of chills. The kind that make me want to pull him in for a kiss and see if he smells as good as I remember.

*Fake relationship. Fake. No sniffing allowed.*

Something tells me I might have to remind myself of this a few more times tonight.

"Thank you, you look great, too." The words sound normal, not like I'm an animal in heat, thank God.

He smiles, and holds out his hand. I stare at it for a minute before I realize he wants me to take it. I do, and our fingers thread together almost naturally.

"I thought we would walk to the restaurant so we can enjoy some wine," he says. How is he so relaxed right now when I'm wound tighter than an antique clock? "Plus, it gives us even more opportunities to be seen together." He turns to me and winks.

"Yeah...sounds good." I stutter out the words, still trying to get over how good it feels doing something as simple as holding his hand.

Jackson fills the walk with conversation, my brain operating on autopilot as I respond. We pass a few people who give us knowing smiles. It's remarkable how easy it is to fool people into thinking we're actually dating.

"Relax, Mila." Jackson's warm breath caresses my ear, and I feel him gently squeeze my hand. "You look like you're walking to your execution, not a date."

"A *fake* date," I whisper back. "Did I mention I hate lying?"

His chuckle reaches me. "Then this was a really stupid idea. Too late now, buttercup."

I stumble to a stop. "Buttercup?"

He shrugs. "Just trying out pet names. You don't like that one? How about *love muffin*. That works with your bakery."

I stare up at him. "Who are you, and what happened to the Jackson that was so standoffish and would only order bran muffins?"

He slings his arm around my shoulder, pulling me in close. "I was corrupted by your apple nut muffins. Was I really that standoffish?"

"Uh, yeah, a little."

A slight frown comes over his face. "Sorry. I guess I was still dealing with everything. Moving here was a big change."

My heart pangs as I remember everything that led to his move. I feel myself soften into his side. "I get it. And I'm glad that you're happy here."

We walk the rest of the way to the restaurant with his arm around my shoulder. When we get there, the hostess shows us to a booth tucked away in the back. A single candle is in the middle of the white tablecloth, and the overall ambiance is one of romance.

"Not great for visibility, but perfect for privacy to discuss the details," Jackson comments.

"Details?" I ask as we sit down in the booth. Jackson slides around so that he's next to me, and after the waiter takes our drink orders, he continues.

"We can tell the truth about how we met, but we need a story for how I asked you out and when, and we need rules for what we're going to do or say to people, that kind of thing."

"You've put a lot of thought into this."

He looks embarrassed by my comment. "Not really, I just figure if we're going to do it, we might as well do it well."

He's right, of course. And somehow, seeing his discomfort makes my own disappear.

"Jackson, I'm teasing. You're right, of course. I propose one formal date a week, hand holding is okay, and we tell people I asked *you* out. What started as me being friendly to the newcomer turned into more when we realized we couldn't keep our hands off each other." I wiggle my eyebrows to show him I'm joking, and it works when I see his shoulders relax.

"Sounds good to me. But I'm going to add on a couple of things. People have seen us kiss. Well, Rosie did, which from what you tell me is as good as the entire town seeing it. Which means we might have to do it again." His eyes darken as he looks at me, and my tongue darts out to lick my lip. Is it hot in here? Or is it just the idea of kissing Jackson again?

"Kissing. Yeah, we can do that."

He nods, slowly, his eyes never leaving my face. I see his gaze flick down to my mouth and up again. The silence grows more and more heated until we're interrupted by the waiter bringing over a bottle of wine.

"Oh, we only ordered a glass each," I say, stopping him from pouring from what looks like a very expensive bottle.

"I know; this is compliments of the Martins." Our waiter gestures across the restaurant to where Turner and Sandra Martin, who own the local hardware store, are smiling and waving at us. My eyes widen and I force a smile and wave back while Jackson chuckles behind me. Just like that, my panic and discomfort over what we are doing is back, and more intense than ever. The waiter pours our wine, and we lift a glass. Jackson nods at the Martins while I'm still blushing furiously.

"Looks like there's even more perks to being your fake boyfriend, Mila Monroe," Jackson murmurs as he takes a sip of wine.

"Oh my God. Jackson." I put my glass down and my hands twist together in my lap. "This is why I hate lying. Oh God, why did I suggest we do this? This is a terrible idea. What are we doing? I can't —"

Jackson's lips cover mine, effectively shutting off my panicked line of thought. My hands still, as one of his covers them and the other cups the nape of my neck. My eyes flutter closed, and for just a second I let myself forget that this is all pretend. But he pulls back all too soon, and I have to stop myself from whimpering at the loss of contact.

"Stop freaking out." He whispers the words against my lips before pressing one more quick kiss against my mouth. Then he backs away and when I open my eyes, he's looking at me over his wineglass, a peculiar expression on his face. Like maybe that kiss affected him just as much as it did me.

# Chapter Eight

*Jackson*

It would be easy to tell myself that I kissed Mila last night to put on a good show for everyone at the restaurant. We need to sell this relationship as real, after all. But the truth is different. The truth is I *wanted* to kiss her. And I enjoyed it. Possibly too much.

I may have been out of the dating scene for a few years, thanks to my ill-fated relationship with Stefani, but I can easily say that my fake date with Mila was better than any real date I can remember going on. After we got over the initial awkward stage, amplified by the Martin's wine gift, everything went great. The conversation flowed, we laughed, we shared food, and touching her felt right. Dropping her off at her house was the worst part, only because I didn't want the night to end. If I have to be in a pretend relationship with anyone, I'm glad it's someone I am at least attracted to, and get along with. I'm glad it's Mila.

I've got the morning off today, but it's an unseasonably cold day. Too cold to hit the water, so I've decided to go on a hike

Mila told me about that's just outside of town. Apparently, there are some hot springs up there, so I tossed some swim shorts into my pack along with some water and snacks, but we'll see. Mostly I just want to get out and have some time to clear my head. I had a message on my phone from my mom, who is still in contact with Stefani's mom. Thankfully, she didn't say anything about my ex, just asked how things were going and reminded me to call her. But even that small piece of contact from home, or my former home, got me thinking about how it all went so fucking wrong.

It has only been a handful of months since Stefani pulled the rug out from underneath my feet. I've spent many nights thinking back over the years we were together, trying to figure out if there were clues or anything that I missed that could have prepared me for her revelation that our relationship was built on lies. I'm not sure if it helps or makes it hurt even more that I cannot think of a damn thing. She had me so well fooled. So convinced that we wanted the same thing — a partnership, a marriage, a life focused on just the two of us and our personal and career aspirations. We talked about all of the trips we would take, the corners of the world we wanted to explore. We shared our dreams and goals and planned out how to support each other. And the entire time, she was holding back, keeping her true desires a secret. She didn't trust me enough to tell me the truth up front. Not only that, but she had so little respect for my wants and opinions that she figured she could convince me to change my mind. Her exact words still haunt me.

*"I didn't think you really meant it. I mean, if you really loved me, you would give me a baby."*

I'm not saying people shouldn't be willing to compromise and change their minds if it's of their own free will. But what she said was nothing short of emotional blackmail. So, I called her bluff.

Thinking about the day I walked away fills me with an unhappy frustration, so I pick up the pace until I'm running up the trail. The incline is significant, but not unmanageable, and the trees offer some shade. Still, I'm certainly breathing heavy when the trail levels out and I come to a clearing. There's tall grass, and large rocks scattered, making me wonder how this place came to be. It looks like it was plucked from the pages of a fairy tale. I half expect woodland creatures to start singing, but instead all I hear is birds chirping and people's voices.

The sight of two men sitting on the ground, bottles of water in hand, brings me to a stop. It's Ethan and Reid. Before I can debate turning around before they see me, Ethan waves me over. I have no idea what he's heard about Mila and I, but I think I'm about to find out.

"Jackson. Good to see you, enjoying your hike?"

"Sure. It's beautiful up here," I reply to Ethan's question.

Reid gestures to the ground beside them. "Take a break with us. We're on our way down, but this fucker made me run sprints up the last section."

"Not my fault your cardio sucks."

"Actually, if you weren't so busy banging Summer, we could be running more often. So it sort of is your fault."

"Fuck off," Ethan says good naturedly before turning to me. "Heard you were out with my sister last night."

I finish swallowing my water, then screw the cap back on my bottle, thinking carefully how to handle this. "I was."

"She deserves to be treated like a queen. You get that, right?" His tone leaves no room for disagreement, not that I would. Mila does deserve the best.

"Absolutely. She's an incredible woman."

He nods slowly, his eyes never leaving mine. "It's good for her to have a man around. She needs someone, especially since, as this asshole said," — he shoves Reid good naturedly — "I'm a bit busier these days with Summer and the resort."

Something about the words he says rubs me the wrong way, and I feel my eyebrows draw together. "I know she's your sister, and you probably know her best, but I gotta say she doesn't strike me as someone who *needs* anyone, much less a man. She's strong, smart, independent, and more than capable of taking care of herself."

Reid barks out a laugh, leaning back and slapping Ethan on the back. "He's got you there, brother!"

After a tense moment, Ethan's face relaxes into a wide smile. "Good answer, man. Good fucking answer."

I let out my breath on a laugh, feeling like I just passed a test I didn't realize I was taking. We talk for a few more minutes, then Ethan and Reid get up and head down the trail, leaving me in the small clearing by myself. I sit there, listening to the birds chirp and the trees rustle in the wind for a while longer before getting up myself and carrying on to the hot springs. The smell of sulphur hits me long before I see the low pools carved into rock. There are a few people using them, none of whom I recognize, but all are friendly enough to wave hello. I don't stay, choosing instead to turn around and head back to the motel to get ready for work.

But as I leave, my mind wanders to Mila in a bikini, sinking into the hot water with me. A hot springs date sounds like a great idea to me.

It's later that week when Mila texts me about viewing the bungalow she has for me to look at. But when I pull up at the small bungalow she isn't there yet, so I take the opportunity to look around. The street is quiet, and all of the houses appear well maintained. Then again, that could be said for all of Dogwood Cove. If this town has a dark side, I haven't found it yet.

The house in front of me is nothing special, but has a nice porch, and a small front yard. There's room in the driveway for two cars, and a big picture window out front. Is it my dream house? No, actually, Mila's place is way closer to what I always imagined wanting for myself. But this place will do just fine for a temporary home until the right thing comes along that's more permanent.

The beep of a car horn makes me turn, and I see Mila pull up. Her dark blue Jeep fits her personality so perfectly, making me think of strength and freedom. She climbs out, her long hair blowing in the gentle breeze, and her smile lights up my own.

"Ready to see your new home?" she calls out cheerfully, dangling a set of keys out in front of her. Apparently her nerves about our fake relationship that were running wild while on our date are gone now, and the confident Mila I first met is back.

"Absolutely." I grin and follow her up to the front door. She unlocks it, then steps back to let me go first. I push open the door, and step into the entryway. The house smells like fresh paint. Mila said Ethan finished up what he wanted to do early, so technically I could move in today if I wanted. Even if the house hadn't suited my needs, I would probably take it just so I could move Harley and I out of the damn motel. But as I wander through to the kitchen, taking in the small back yard, I know I'll be going straight from here to the motel to pack up my clothes and move in.

"You said it's fully furnished, so all of this stays?" I ask, resting my hand on the back of a surprisingly comfortable looking chair that sits beside the front window. Guaranteed my cat is going to claim that spot as his own.

"Yup. Everything you see is included. All you need are some fresh linens and yourself."

"It's perfect, Mila. Thank you." When my gaze reaches her, she's blushing. Suddenly I find myself wondering just how far that adorable pink colour goes, as it disappears underneath the V-neck of her shirt.

"It's no big deal. Just renting a house to a friend." The fist bump she gives my shoulder makes me frown, as does the way she says *friend*. It shouldn't, that's what we are, after all. "Okay, so here's the keys. I have to get back to the bakery. Just drop off your deposit and rent cheques with Ethan when you can."

"Not with you?"

Her blush deepens as she darts her gaze up to meet mine. "Umm, no. It seemed weird, seeing as we're meant to be dating and all, to have you give me money. And since Ethan and I co-own the house, you can just pay him."

Her answer makes sense, but something tells me she's also trying to put some separation between us. Which gives me a weird pang in my chest. Must be because I'm worried what Morton will say if our relationship ends too soon. *Or maybe it's because I really like spending time with her.* Sure, I can admit that she's a great friend. And our first fake date was a success. That kiss at the restaurant was...well, that was more than a success. That was something I'm not ready to fully think about just yet.

"Okay. Well, thanks for showing it to me." I put my hands in my pockets and lean against the back of the couch. "We should plan our next date."

"Right. There's the Canada Day celebration on Monday, we could go to that together."

July first. That means I've been in Dogwood Cove for just over two months. It feels like it's been so much longer.

"Sounds good, lots of public exposure. Are you ready for me to kiss you in front of everyone?" I'm teasing, but a part of me really wants to see her response. And the momentary flare of heat in her eyes tells me I'm not the only one who's thinking about our kiss from the other night.

"Bring it on. Just be ready for my brother to go all overprotective on you."

I laugh at that. "Oh, he and Reid already did that when I ran into them while hiking to the hot springs the other day."

Mila groans. "Seriously? Ah, crap. I'm sorry, I was joking. I didn't really think he would say anything." She drops her face into her hands, and I reach out to gently take her wrists and pull her arms down.

"Mila, relax. He didn't say anything bad. It was good, exactly what your brother should do when you start dating someone. He loves you."

"Ugh. I know he does. I just wish he would back off a little. He doesn't need to be so worried about me and my personal life."

Somehow, my hands are still on her wrists, and I realize my thumbs are tracing gentle circles around her skin. I don't think about what I'm doing, just tug her closer until she's close enough for me to wrap my arms around her shoulders. Her head falls to my chest and I have to remind myself I'm just being a friend. But...would friends hug like this? And enjoy it...a lot? *Only if you want more than friendship.* My inner voice needs to shut the fuck up right now, because she feels good in my arms, and she certainly doesn't seem like she thinks this is weird.

"That's the whole point of what we're doing, though, isn't it? Show your brother he doesn't need to worry about you, even if it is stupid that it takes a relationship for that to happen."

"Just like it's stupid that Morton won't believe that you're settled in town unless you're in a relationship?"

I reluctantly take a step back, letting my hands drop down to my sides. "Exactly. It's all so ridiculous, but as long as you and I know what we're doing and why, it'll work."

"Just don't fall for me, Jackson Holt."

I scoff at her teasing. "I could say the same to you, Mila Monroe."

"No chance. You might be handsome and have sexy forearms, but I don't have time for love."

She doesn't have the time, and my heart still feels too jaded to even consider it. On paper, we look like the perfect pairing for a relationship of convenience.

And yet it stings to hear those words.

# Chapter Nine

*Mila*

"If you want to knock down that wall, we could, but not all the way across. We'll need a structural beam as well. Mila, are you even listening to me?"

Ethan's frustrated voice interrupts my distracted thoughts, and I look at him guiltily. "Yeah. A beam. Okay."

"No, it's not just 'okay'. A beam is a lot of work, and a lot of money. What's going on Mills, you're the one who wanted to meet today, so why are you so distracted?"

I can't tell him the truth, that I haven't been able to stop thinking about Jackson. When he pulled me into his arms at the house yesterday, it didn't feel like a friend comforting a friend. It felt like more. Even if the words we spoke said otherwise, my damn heart is starting to see him differently. Blame the kiss at the restaurant, blame the funny texts we keep sending each other, blame the way my breath speeds up when he walks into the bakery each morning and kisses my forehead for everyone to see.

He might be a fake boyfriend but he's a damn good one.

"Sorry, Ethan. I'm just tired." I hate lying to my brother most of all, and he knows I'm terrible at it, so for a minute, I think he's going to call me out on it. But I'm not faking the dark circles under my eyes, those are courtesy of waking up before five am six days a week. I'm looking forward to this week when I get two days off, thanks to the Canada Day holiday falling on a Monday, the day after my usual day off. My friends tell me I work too much and I'm starting to think they're right. Not that I can admit that now, especially as Ethan and I are finally figuring out my plans for expansion. It's taken years for me to save up the money for this, and for the space to be available. But here I am, standing in what will eventually become the café side of The Nutty Muffin.

I hope my mom is happy.

"So, we add a beam. I've got the budget for it, right?"

Ethan looks at me for a second before answering. "Yeah, you do. I still think it might be easier if we don't knock down the entire wall. Just part of it. It'll feel open but have some separation. You said you wanted one side to be more of a deli or café, so then maybe the other side stays focused on the bakery. You could add more display cases if you move seating over here."

I look around the space, trying to envision what he's suggesting. And I can see it easily. Instead of only offering pre-made sandwiches like I do right now, on a very limited basis at that, I could have this side of the space be where customers could sit and eat, with staff making sandwiches on my baked bread, fresh to order. Then the other side could be for all things sweet.

"Do you think the name still works? Can a lunch place be called The Nutty Muffin?"

Ethan chuckles. "I think if you tried to change the name, you'd have a riot on your hands."

That makes me smile, mostly because it's true. My regulars love the name of the bakery, some have even asked if I could make mugs with the logo on it. Paige sketched the adorable muffin with a cute face for me, and I have to admit, it would look perfect on a mug or a shirt.

"Okay, the name stays for now, but I'm not totally convinced. We knock down part of the wall, add a beam, more display cases next door, and a food prep area over here. Can we still expand the kitchen?"

Ethan and I walk to the back of the space, where he takes some measurements before confirming I have room back here for at least an oven and refrigerator, plus some storage. The majority of the baking will still happen on the other side, but it'll be nice to have a little work space here.

When we're finished, we wander over to the bakery where things are slow but steady, as usual for the early afternoon. Ethan pours us both a cup of coffee while I go to the back and grab two raspberry scones that I made fresh this morning with raspberries from a local farm. In the summer, I'm overwhelmed with choices of fresh fruit to use in my treats, and berry scones sell out every single day. I happen to know they're my brother's favourite, which is why I saved these for him.

"You're too good to me, Mills," he groans when he sees the plate.

"Yeah, well, you can thank me in labour next door."

"I will as soon as I finish up at the resort." Crumbs fall from his mouth as he speaks, and I roll my eyes.

"You're disgusting."

He just grins and keeps on devouring the scone until there's nothing left. When he's done, Ethan settles back in his chair with his coffee in hand.

"Do we need to talk about Jackson Holt?" he asks casually.

"Nope. Definitely not. And I heard about you and Reid interrogating him the other day."

He has the decency to look at least a little chagrined. "It wasn't really an interrogation, Mills. Just a guy asking his little sister's new boyfriend a few questions."

"How is that *not* an interrogation, Ethan?" I fold my arms across my chest and glare at him. I'm not actually that upset, seeing as Jackson assured me it was no big deal, but I'll be damned if I'm going to pass up the opportunity to give my brother a hard time.

"Look. It's my job as your big brother to look out for you. And that means making sure the man you're seeing is good enough for you and has the right intentions."

"What is this, the dark ages? Pretty sure I can judge for myself if he's good enough. And what exactly would be the right intentions? We're dating. Not getting married."

Ethan throws his hands up in defeat and I fight back a smile of triumph. "Hey, woah, settle down there, Miss Defensive. I'm sorry for being an involved sibling."

"It's okay, Ethan. Thanks for looking out for me."

Ethan's face softens. "I love you, Mills."

"Love you, too."

He leans forward slightly. "For what it's worth, he passed interrogation with flying colours."

Before I can ask Ethan exactly what he means by *that* statement, he stands up to leave. "I gotta go meet Summer at the resort; see you for dinner Saturday? You could bring Jackson if you want."

Pretending to be together in front of Ethan and Summer feels daunting right now, so I just make a noncommittal sound of agreement and watch as he heads out the door. I know we will be in front of them, and many more on Monday at the celebrations, but that seems like a lot less pressure than dinner with just the four of us. I'll have to talk to Jackson about coming up with a good reason for his absence. I pull out my phone to text him, and find a message already waiting from him.

**JACKSON: I just had Mrs. Svenson tell me I need to treat you well or she'll sic her son on me. Apparently he's some kind of military sniper? Please tell me she's joking...**

**MILA: LOL nope, she isn't. He really is. But he's stationed in Ontario, so you're safe.**

**JACKSON: This town is very protective of you…**

**MILA: What can I say, I'm a popular person. I've won them over with muffins.**

**JACKSON: Everyone does seem to love your muffins.**

**JACKSON: That sounds dirty. Sorry.**

**MILA: It's okay, I get it *winking emoji***

**MILA: Hey, if my brother asks you about coming to dinner on Saturday can you pretend that you're busy?**

**JACKSON: Sure, but why?**

**MILA: I'll explain later.**

I bite the end of my thumb, hoping he won't push for a better explanation. It's weird trying to figure out how to tell him over text that I'm worried I won't be able to pretend very well in front of Ethan and Summer. The truth is, being around Jackson is easy. Heck, being affectionate with Jackson is easy. I think I'm more worried about lying in front of my brother. The less of that I have to deal with, the better.

**JACKSON: Okay. Want to grab some pizza tonight and hang out at my place? Wow. I have a place. Thanks again for hooking me up with the house. I moved everything in today.**

**MILA: Sounds good. And you're welcome – I'm glad it worked out.**

**JACKSON: Great. Come on by around 6.**

Friends can eat pizza together. Friends who are pretending to be more *should* eat pizza together. If someone sees me going to his house at night, that's a good thing.

Right?

Unfortunately, the idea of being alone with Jackson doesn't feel like a good thing for long. In fact, as my day goes on, and I close up the bakery and head for Serena's studio where the four of us girls are going to do a yoga class with Summer teaching us, my brain starts going crazy, wondering if my going to his house tonight is actually a stupid idea.

The man is hot. Like seriously hot. And I really like kissing him. Even if so far, our kisses have all been for show, it'll be hard to resist feeling those lips against mine again.

I'm in the middle of flowing from downward dog into pigeon pose when I lose balance and fall to the side. Serena looks up with an exasperated huff, and Summer lifts her head from her perfect posture.

"Mila, what's going on? You're so distracted today."

"Trust me, you're not the first person to tell me that," I reply drily, remembering Ethan's frustration earlier.

"If this is what sex does to you, maybe you should go back to being single. You're going to become a liability in the kitchen if this keeps up."

That observation comes from the ever-pragmatic Paige, and I have to stop myself from blurting out the truth. That I am still single, that it's all a big lie, but that I'm distracted by thinking of what might happen tonight.

Nothing is going to happen.

Correction, I can't *let* anything happen. Not only because I'm too busy to date anyone for real and use up the emotional and mental energy it would take to maintain a relationship, but because Jackson has made it abundantly clear he doesn't want to be with anyone right now. Which means letting something pesky like my attraction to his kisses get in the way will only make things weird.

"I'm not having sex, you guys. We just started dating. I've just got a lot on my mind with the expansion, that's all." I ignore their curious glances, and make my way back to downward dog, this time flowing my leg through into pigeon pose properly. Closing my eyes, I focus inward on my breathing, and try to shut out all of the crazy thoughts and feelings that are swirling around in my head.

When our class is finished, the four of us sit around the studio on our mats chatting. I love how seamlessly Summer has fit into my group of friends, as if she never left town and we never lost touch. A pang of guilt over lying to them about Jackson hits me, but I forcibly move it aside. They won't understand why I'm doing this, why I feel this pressure to pretend I'm happily in a relationship. Even though Summer is the only one of us currently paired off, the other two often bug me about working too much as well. They don't see that getting the bakery, and now the café side also up and running is my top priority. Sure, I complain about the lack of single men in Dogwood Cove as much as they do. But that doesn't mean I actually want a boyfriend. I'm content on my own, focusing on my business, and living life my way.

"Jackson's coming to dinner on Saturday, right?" Summer asks quietly as we're rolling up our mats. Every Saturday, Ethan and I used to get together for dinner. It expanded to include Summer when she came back to town, because growing up she was as close as family to us. I can't dodge the question as easily as I did with Ethan earlier, so I opt for a vague response, hoping it's good enough.

"I'm not really sure what his schedule is like. Besides, its early. He doesn't need to do the whole 'dinner with the family' thing right away."

"Oh, come on, Mila, it's us. We're family, but we're also all friends. He had better be okay hanging out with us," she chides.

"Of course he is. We'll be at Canada Day together," I'm quick to respond, not wanting to give her any reason to question things. "I just have to check what his plans are on Saturday. That's all."

Summer's perceptive, and I'm a crap liar, so she's looking at me skeptically.

"Is everything okay, Mila?"

"Of course," I force out a light laugh. "Why wouldn't it be? I've got a great boyfriend, great friends, a great job, everything is great. I'm great."

Even I can hear how ridiculous that sounds, and judging by Summer's raised eyebrows, she hears it, too.

"Sounds great," she says, her voice laced with sarcasm. But her face softens as she continues, "You know you can talk to me about anything, right?"

I smile at her, and the worry fades from her face. "I love you for caring, but I'm seriously fine. I just don't know if Jackson is free on Saturday, that's all."

She pulls me in for a hug. "Okay. Good. I'm happy for you. It's nice to see you doing something other than work."

"Hey, I do plenty of other things. Book club, yoga, dinners with you guys."

"Okay, okay, I get it. But you also work a lot. Six days a week, twelve hours a day sometimes. It's good to have someone out there taking care of you, that's all." Summer gives me one final squeeze.

"Thanks." I pull back, hating the guilt I feel over lying through my teeth to one of my best friends. The fact that she doesn't question what I'm saying makes me feel worse, not better. Apparently, I'm not such a bad liar if she believes me so quickly.

Fake dating Jackson was meant to make life easier.

So why does it suddenly feel like everything is way more complicated, and way more stressful than before?

# CHAPTER TEN

*Jackson*

Being friends with a woman is a new experience for me, and I like the fact that Mila seems just as happy with pizza at home as she is with a nice dinner out. As soon as she got to the house, we ordered some food, then chatted casually until it arrived. She's got big plans for the expansion of her bakery, and I admire her drive. I'm the same way with my career, and it's kind of nice to be able to talk with someone who gets the level of dedication I feel. When the food arrives, we load up our plates, each grab a beer, and head out onto the back deck to sit down. Harley meanders out after us, and flops onto his side in a patch of sunshine.

"That is the laziest cat I've ever seen." Mila giggles as Harley rolls onto his back, like the sunseeker he is.

"Yeah, you got that right. He won't even bother trying to chase a bird or anything. Give the cat a warm spot or a patch of sunshine and he won't move for hours."

She bends down and strokes the fur on Harley's stomach. *I'm jealous of my cat.* For fuck's sake, why am I wanting to feel her hands on me? Things changed between us yesterday when I hugged her. It wasn't for show, it was just because I wanted to, I don't know, comfort her? Sure. I'll go with that. The problem is, it felt so damn good having her in my arms. I pick up my beer and take a long drink, focusing on the feel of the cool liquid sliding down my throat, hoping it will kill some of the heat inside of me. When I tip my head back down, I catch her staring at me, but she looks away quickly. She picks up a piece of pizza and takes a bite, chewing with her eyes closed and a small smile.

"I'm so glad you're not a weirdo who eats fruit on pizza." She licks sauce off her fingertips, and I stifle a groan.

"I'll eat almost anything on pizza, but anchovies and pineapple are just wrong." I keep my eyes focused on my plate, closing them briefly as she lets out another hum of satisfaction. Does she even know that everything she does is fucking sexy? It's becoming harder and harder, pun intended, to remind myself that all we share is friendship. Anything more needs to be saved for when we're out in public, and need to convince people there's something between us.

"Agreed." Mila sits back in her chair and lets out a contented sigh.

"You seem like you're feeling a lot more relaxed about everything than you were yesterday."

She tilts her head, and a small smile crosses her face. "Am I? That's funny, because I was freaking out earlier about how complicated this is, lying to everyone. But then I come here, and I feel totally fine."

Something about that makes me sit up a little taller. I like the fact that she feels good around me. "What you're saying is, you can't resist me and my forearms?"

Mila's head falls back and a carefree laugh bubbles out of her. "Oh God, I never should have admitted my attraction to your forearms."

"But you did, and now I'll never let you forget it." I grin and flex my arms out in front of me, earning another laugh. She leans over and slaps my arm gently.

"Stop it. Arrogance is not a good look on anyone."

I chuckle and stand up, taking her plate. "Do you want some more pizza?"

"Sure." She smiles up at me.

I head back inside and serve up another slice for each of us. Placing my hands on the kitchen counter, I drop my head and take a deep breath. I know it's just physical attraction, nothing more, but seeing Mila relaxed and happy, it's making me want things I don't know if I should want.

"Jackson? Is everything okay?"

I look up to see Mila standing in the doorway, holding our beer bottles and looking at me with uncertainty painted on her face. I smile quickly.

"Yeah, of course. Need another beer?"

She nods and walks over to me. But instead of going to the fridge for another drink, she puts the bottles down and crosses her arms.

"Liar."

"Mila," I say as she takes a step closer, dropping her arms to her sides. My hand is gripping the countertop.

"Do you know why I feel so good when I'm around you?"

"Why?" I ask hoarsely.

"Because being around you feels right. Natural. Normal. I don't have to pretend when I'm with you, I can just be me." She comes to a stop only inches away from me, and I want so fucking badly to touch her. I don't know what's going on right now, but whatever spell we're under, I don't want it to break.

"I can do what I want to do. And I know you understand me." Her words have barely registered before I feel her lips on mine. They brush softly together, then she speaks again. "I can kiss you, and I know you won't push me for more." Our lips touch again. "We can call it practice if you want. All I know is I really want to kiss you again."

"*Fuck. Mila.*" Her name comes out as a growl this time as I capture her mouth with mine. Her fingers tunnel into my hair, gripping my head closer and I take our kiss deeper. The raging desire inside of me is growing hotter and hotter. I want this woman; I need this woman. Any logic and reasoning that says this is a bad idea has disappeared, and pure lust is left in its place. I could blame it on not having sex for almost eight months, but the truth is, it's Mila. My body wants her, craves her. And even if sex isn't on the table for us right now, I realize I want it to be, and soon.

But not yet.

Right now, I just want to kiss her.

I slant my mouth to cover more of hers. Her tongue slicks across my lips and I open, letting us tangle together. Soft moans come from somewhere, and I realize it's her. The sound makes my cock stir in my shorts, and I know she feels it because she presses her hips against me. Fuck. It's too much, too soon. I have to pump the brakes on this before it goes too far.

I pull back. Both of us are breathing heavily. Mila's hands drop to my shoulders, and my hands are still holding her waist.

"Wow."

"Yeah. Wow." My words come out rough.

She lets her hands slide down my body until they drop to her sides and I instantly miss the contact.

"I should go," she says quietly, stepping back, and forcing my hands to leave her hips.

"Are you sure?"

"Yeah." She smiles up at me, then walks around to the other side of the counter to gather her things. "Thanks for dinner, and" — she waves her hand around, biting her lip — "this."

I look at her closely, trying to see if there is any sign of remorse for kissing me. Thankfully there's none, so I take her leaving for what I assume it is. A step back, re-establishing boundaries. Good thing she can't read my mind right now, because all I want to do is smash those boundaries to rubble.

Instead, I walk her to the door.

"I'll see you for breakfast tomorrow."

Her eyes twinkle at me. "Yeah. I'll save you a bran muffin."

As I watch Mila drive away, I realize something. She's changing more than just my breakfast habits. She's changing me. I don't feel like the angry, jaded man I was when I first came here. I feel happy, content, and hopeful. Three things I haven't felt for a very long time.

Canada Day is hot and sunny. When I pick Mila up, I'm glad for my sunglasses because I know my eyes widen in appreciation of the tight red shorts she's wearing with a white and red tank top. Her long hair is pulled up in a high ponytail, and she's got sandals on her feet, showing off bright red toenails.

"Someone's taking their national pride seriously," I tease as I walk up to her. She walks down the path, putting an extra sway into her hips as if she's on the runway.

"If I'm going to celebrate Canada's birthday, I'm doing it right. Where's your red?" she asks, putting her hand on my arm to turn me around, as if I might have some hidden colour on my back.

"Sorry to disappoint, no red." I look down at my light grey T-shirt and black shorts with a shrug of my shoulders.

"Well, we need to fix that. We'll find something at one of the booths, I'm sure."

I raise my eyebrows. "No tacky tourist shit, please."

Mila rolls her eyes at me. "Fine. Nothing too tacky."

The celebration takes up all of the town square and surrounding streets, which have been shut down for the day. I take Mila's hand as we walk down the street, the sounds of people laughing and music playing growing louder as we approach.

"Wouldn't it be good business if you were open today?" I ask as I notice several of the businesses that line the square open and bustling with customers.

"Yeah, but I've been coming to the Dogwood Cove Canada Day party since I was born. Maybe in the future I'll have a manager that can run the bakery, but for now I'm the one in charge and I don't want to work today."

"Makes sense to me," I reply. That's the last chance we get to talk, just the two of us, because as soon as we reach the crowd, we're swept up by people greeting us. I know I have to get used to how involved these people are in everyone's lives; that's the reality of a small town. Doctor Morton tried to warn me about that. But I can't get over how *many* people come up to us, commenting on how good we apparently look together, and how happy Mila looks. I feel her grip on my hand grow tighter, and her smile grow less genuine, and I realize she's uncomfortable. Thinking quickly, I excuse us from whoever is talking; honestly, I've lost track of who everyone is at this point, and we walk quickly over to the front of the bakery.

"Do you have the key with you?"

"Of course I do," she says, looking at me, confused. "But why?"

"Just open the door. It'll look like we're sneaking away for a minute, which we are, but not for whatever reason they assume we are."

She opens the door, and we step into the cool, dimly lit bakery. I pull her straight through to the kitchen, away from any prying eyes out front.

"Now. Breathe."

Mila lets out a huff of relief and sags against the counter. "How could you tell I needed a minute?"

"Because you were cutting off the circulation to my hand," I reply with a teasing grin.

She winces and I squeeze her hand gently, so she knows I'm not upset. "Sorry. It's just a lot, you know? Why do I magically look happier with you beside me? What was wrong with me before?"

She sinks down onto a stool and lets her head fall onto the counter. I come behind her and start to gently massage her shoulders.

"There was nothing wrong with you before, and there's nothing wrong with you right now. Some people just have an idea in their head about what happiness should look like, and when you don't meet that expectation, they don't know how to handle it."

She lifts her head and turns, forcing my hands to drop away. "Exactly." She studies me for a minute, our eyes locked on each other. "It's kind of crazy how you get it. Not many people do."

*Not many people feel the way we do.* I think it but don't say it. Because saying it would mean trusting her, trusting that she understands me, and wants the same things. And if a woman as incredible as Mila actually wants the same things out of life that I do, that would be...yeah. That would be something.

"Feel ready to face the hordes again?" I ask, effectively diffusing the weird emotional moment. Mila stands up and takes an exaggerated breath in and out.

"As ready as I'll ever be." She sticks out her hand, and I take it, threading our fingers together. We walk back to the front of the bakery and out into the hot summer day. The difference in Mila is noticeable. She's not hunching forward; she's standing up tall, confident, happy. And I know it has nothing to do with me by her side, and everything to do with her remembering she doesn't have to hinge her happiness on other people's expectations. She is perfect exactly the way she is.

She really is.

We wander around some more, and this time when people stop and comment, Mila is quick with a reply, redirecting the conversation adeptly when she wants to. I take a backseat and let her lead, making sure to stay appropriately connected and affectionate, but not crossing any lines. Which is why it comes as a surprise when she stops me in the middle of the sidewalk, and steps in front of me, and lifts up to kiss me. I kiss her back, mentally assuming someone's watching. Then again, our kiss at my house wasn't because someone was watching.

"Thank you," she says, dropping back onto her heels and smiling at me.

"For what?"

"Just for being you, for going along with all of this, and for making it a lot easier than it would have been with anyone else."

Her words do something to me, making me feel weird inside, so I decide to squash them with an attempt at humour. "Are you saying you would have tried this with someone else if I wasn't around? Wow, and here I was feeling special."

Her laugh is everything I wanted in that instant. "Oh, you're special, Jackson. Very special." She punctuates her words with a waggle of her eyebrows, and I chuckle. "Now, come on. We still need to find you the perfect T-shirt."

Five minutes later, Mila has somehow convinced me to buy a bright red shirt with a white maple leaf on it and 'Eh?' written underneath. It's tacky. But believe it or not, it's the least tacky shirt we could find.

"Just put it on, Jackson. Get into the spirit of things." She's holding it up in front of me, and the excitement on her face would be enough to make me do a dance in the middle of the street if she asked me to.

"Fine. Hand it over," I say, pulling my shirt off. When my head is free, I catch her unabashedly staring at me, and fuck, is she licking her lips? "Like what you see?"

Her eyes widen and she blushes furiously. "Oh, stop it. Put a damn shirt on."

I do, but I do it slowly, tightening my abs as I drag the stiff, cheap fabric over my body. My eyes don't leave Mila's face, and I hear a hitch in her breath that makes my dick stir in my pants. When we're ready to go, I don't take her hand. I wrap my arm around her waist and tuck her closely into my side. Close enough that I can bend down and whisper in her ear.

"There's no rule saying you can't look at my body, Mila. Because if there was, I've broken it a thousand times by now because I can't stop looking at your ass in those shorts."

# Chapter Eleven

*Mila*

If there was a prize for most turned on at a Canada Day celebration, I would win. After his comment about my ass, Jackson didn't whisper anything else even remotely dirty, but he didn't have to. His hand on my hips, or shoulder, or holding mine, was enough. The way he knew when I needed a break from everything, and took me to the bakery and rubbed my shoulders made me damn near swoon. For a fake boyfriend, he's doing a bang-up job.

But my nerves were still shot by the end of the day. Hanging out with my brother and all of my friends while pretending to be head over heels for Jackson wasn't the hard part. After all, I *am* ridiculously attracted to the guy. It's more the fact that the entire time I knew we were lying.

I fell asleep quickly last night, and it was one of those deep, dreamless sleeps that should leave you feeling so refreshed and energized the next morning. Instead, I feel like I'm hungover as I stumble into my kitchen, mind set on one thing: coffee.

I'm beyond relieved that the bakery is closed, because I'm pretty sure I would do something stupid like overwhip the cream for the pastries and end up with chunky butter if I tried to bake anything today. Thank God for small mercies — last night I remembered to set up the coffee maker on its usual "day off" alarm, so the pot is fresh and steaming. I pour a mug, top it off with cream and brown sugar the way I like it, and make my way into my living room. Milo comes in from outside through the open back door and climbs up on the couch beside me. I wiggle my feet underneath his body, enjoying the comfortable weight of him.

The near silence, interrupted only by the sounds of birds chirping outside, is perfection. I feel the leftover stress from yesterday slowly seep out of my body. I'm mid-sip when Milo lifts his head up and lets out a woof. Seconds later, there's a knock on my front door.

"Good boy," I say, ruffling the fur on the top of his head. I get up, and he jumps down off the couch with me. The ease with which he moves now makes me smile. We go to open the door together, and when Milo sees Jackson standing outside, his whole rear end starts to wiggle excitedly. *Pretty sure my butt would wiggle with excitement, too, if it wouldn't make me look crazy.* Jackson bends down to give Milo some love and the two of them end up in a pile on my front porch. Eventually he looks up at me with a grin.

"Oh, hey Mila."

I cross my arms and arch my brow at him. "'Oh, hey Mila'? That's all I get? The dog gets more of a greeting than I do?"

He slowly stands up, and when he does, I take in an audible breath at how close he is and the heat radiating from his eyes.

"Hi, Mila." Those are the only words of warning I get before he leans down and presses a soft kiss to my cheek. It's sweet, and way too short, and I want more. So much more. Jackson must sense this, because he looks at me closely for a second, then his head dips down again and his lips meet mine. There's nothing sweet about this kiss, and it goes on and on, until our arms are wrapped around each other, and we're pressed as close together as humanly possible. And it still isn't enough. We fumble inside, Jackson pushing the door closed as I try not to climb him like a tree. Our lips are fused together, and my brain is spiraling with pleasure.

Somehow we make it to my couch, and Jackson lowers me down slowly before moving on top of me. His weight settles onto me, our bodies lining up perfectly. My hips start to rock up into him in time with his kisses. His hand is tangled in my hair, and the occasional tug on the strands sends lightning bolts of arousal straight down my spine. It's full steam ahead for whatever's going to happen next, until my brain gets in the way.

*What the hell are we doing.*

"Stop." I push at his chest, and like the perfect gentleman he is, Jackson immediately backs off.

"Sorry, I...shit." He runs his hands through his hair, messing it up even more than I already had in my crazed passion. I can tell he's feeling guilty for what just happened, which is ridiculous, since I was as much a part of it as he was.

"No, don't apologize. I want this. I want you, trust me. I just think maybe we should take a minute and talk about whatever we're about to do?"

Jackson sits back against the couch. "Yeah. We should. And I am sorry to have just taken you like that, I don't know what came over me."

I gesture down at my sleep shorts and tank top. "Clearly, you were overwhelmed by my sexy outfit and bedhead."

Finally he laughs, and the tension is gone. "Maybe pajamas turn me on, did you think about that?"

I grin. "My mistake. Next time I'll answer the door naked."

Lord, the smoulder he gives me at that comment just about makes me faint. "That wouldn't exactly help my self-control, Mila."

I stand up. "I need more coffee before we talk about whatever this was." I wave my hand between us without meeting his eyes. Walking into my kitchen, I feel him behind me. And when I reach up into the cabinet to get down a second mug, he's right there. His hands come to the counter on either side of me, penning me in. I don't turn around, letting the energy between us bounce from him to me.

"What are we doing, Jackson," I say quietly. His head drops to my shoulder, and after a second he presses a kiss to the bare skin there.

"I don't know. All I know is that I want you, more than I expected to. And every time I see you, it gets harder and harder to resist."

Slowly I turn to face him. There's an intoxicating combination of desire and vulnerability in his expression, and when I reach up to cup his stubble-covered cheek, his eyes close and he presses into my hand.

"Why do we need to resist?"

His low chuckle is full of need. "I've been asking myself the same damn question."

I take a deep breath before I take the inevitable plunge. "So, maybe we don't. Resist anymore, that is." I watch him carefully as I continue. "Maybe we modify our arrangement slightly. Fake dating, real sex."

His eyes flare wide. "Are you sure you're okay with that?"

To answer him, I wind my arms around his neck, letting my fingers tunnel into his hair as I pull him back down. Right before our lips collide, I whisper softly, "Absolutely."

Jackson lets out a sound of pure lust as his hands drop down to my ass. Then suddenly I'm airborne as he lifts me up onto the counter I was just pressed against. His grip moves to my knees, which he pushes apart so he can step in between, and he slides me forward so that I'm flush with his body. I can feel the rock hard length of his erection straining against the soft fabric of the shorts he's wearing, and the sensation elicits a moan of arousal from me that sounds primal.

His hands slide up and down the sides of my body, dipping under my tank top. On the next breath his thumbs reach the sides of my bare breasts.

"Christ, Mila, no bra?"

I shake my head as his fingers slide around to tease my nipples. There is no way I can formulate any more of a response right now, so I just moan and thrust my chest into his hands. He lifts my shirt over my head and tosses it somewhere behind him before lowering his head to suck my breast into his mouth.

I'm lost.

The waves of sensation wash over me, making me dizzy with desire. He licks, nips and sucks at my nipples until I'm desperate, keening with desire. I've never been this turned on just from someone playing with my breasts, but it's Jackson, and everything he does turns me on. Everything.

My hands grab at his shirt, impatiently tugging it up. He breaks away from me just long enough to take it off, freeing up all of those tawny colored muscles for me to run my hands over as he returns his lips to my chest, licking a swath between the slopes of my breasts before circling around my nipples again.

"God, Jackson," I gasp as he gently nips at my skin. His lips travel down my stomach, bringing goosebumps to my skin everywhere he touches. When he reaches the edge of my shorts, he lifts his head, his eyes burning into mine.

"I need to know if you taste as sweet as I think you do."

Breathless and speechless, I nod. His fingers hook into the sides of my shorts and I lift my hips up enough for him to slide them down. The cold of the stone countertop makes me gasp when my sensitized skin hits it, but the chill is erased by pure heat when Jackson bends down, and I feel his warm breath against my sex.

"Fuck yes," he growls just before swiping his tongue up the length of my slit. My head falls back, and I prop myself up with my hands as he stokes the fire burning inside of me higher and higher. He presses his tongue flat against me, exerting just the right amount of pressure and one of my hands flies to his head to hold him there.

I start to breathe heavier and faster as my release starts to build. The man is a fucking genius with his mouth, and a small part of my brain wonders how the hell his ex ever managed to walk away from this. I don't realize his hands have moved from my hips, where he was holding me so tightly I'm pretty sure I'll have fingerprint bruises there tomorrow, until I feel two thick fingers sliding into me. His thumb moves in a circle on my clit, two fingers thrust in and out, and *oh fuck*, there's his tongue again, too.

"Oh my God. Oh God. Oh Jackson. There. Don't stop. Yes. Yes. Yes." My words turn into a garbled mess as I cry out, overtaken by the most intense orgasm I have ever had. If it weren't for the cabinet behind me holding me up right now, I would collapse. Eventually the waves of my release subside, and I become aware of the fact that I'm sitting on my kitchen counter, completely naked.

I blink open my eyes to see Jackson staring at me intently.

"You're stunning when you come."

Somehow, I find the ability to speak. "Maybe we could make it happen again?" I loop my arms around his neck and pull him forward so I can kiss him. I can taste myself on his lips, but it only makes me want him even more. And clearly, he feels the same way, because he slides his hands under my ass and lifts me into his arms.

"Where's the bedroom?"

I point in the direction of the hallway that leads to my room, and he takes off for it, his long legs eating up the distance.

My bed is still a mess from last night, but he doesn't seem to care as he lays me down, coming over top of me just as he did on the couch earlier. When I push at his chest again, confusion mars his handsome face. Until, that is, he rolls off of me and I immediately move to straddle his hips. I bend down, letting my long hair fall around us. Jackson reaches his hand up to gather it away from my face, gently tugging my face down so he can kiss me deeply, like he needs me more than air to breathe. We grind on top of each other, our bare skin slick with heat. It's the hottest make out session of my life, and I know it's only going to get hotter.

I pull back and lean over to open the top drawer of my bedside table. It may have been a stupidly long time since I had sex, but a girl's gotta be prepared. I take out a strip of condoms and toss them on the bed.

When my eyes meet his again, I realize I might need more protection than a small circle of latex. I might need to protect my heart before he finds a way through all of my defenses.

"Just remember, don't fall for me." My joke falls flat on my ears, but Jackson just quirks his lips at me before sitting up, using one hand to grip the back of my neck while the other slides down to my hip. He presses me in tighter against his body, and my body starts to writhe on top of him once again as he kisses me. His lips are a drug that I don't mind being addicted to. After a minute or so— but who's counting — I bring my hands to the button on his shorts. When they're open, I slide them down, taking his boxers with them, watching shamelessly as his cock springs free.

Holy. Shit.

It's long, and thick, and perfect. I lick my lips with anticipation, and Jackson groans.

"Fuck. Don't do that, Mila."

"Do what?" I grin at him wickedly, and do it again, taking my time, making sure my tongue caresses every corner of my lips.

With a growl he grabs me by the hips and suddenly I'm on my back again, with his hard length pressed against me.

"Please tell me you're okay with hard and fast, because it's been a while, darlin', and you've got me ready to explode with how fucking sexy you are."

"Yes. Now." I push the strangled words past my lips as I writhe underneath his hands that are traveling up and down my body. I reach down and take his cock in my hand, stroking it once, twice, then notching it at my entrance. My sex is slick with arousal, and he slides through my folds easily, but that's not enough. I need to feel him inside of me. As deep as he can go.

I don't need words to communicate right now, my body does all the talking for me. I open my hips wide and lift my legs to wrap around Jackson's waist. His tip penetrates me, but he's holding back. My hands go to his ass, and I squeeze. His lips move from my neck to my mouth, and as he kisses me, he plunges in and my hips rise to meet him.

Jackson stills, his cock so far inside it feels like we are one. "Mila," he whispers my name almost reverently, and I swear his eyes can see into my soul. I didn't expect it to feel this intense; this is meant to just be sex between friends. Nothing more. But there are dangerous feelings being stirred up inside of me. I close my eyes and start to move underneath him, hoping he'll get the message. I need this to just be physical. I need to keep my heart out of it.

With every stroke of his cock, I feel my control slipping a little bit more. He reaches down and lifts one of my legs up and over his shoulder, and the change in position makes me shriek out his name. He pounds into me, and I can feel every inch of him touching me, burning me.

"Jackson. Ohmygod. Jackson. Yes. Yes. Yes. Ahhhh!"

I grab at the sheets beside me, my back arching as my body takes over. And when Jackson bends down and pulls my breast into his mouth, sucking it hard, I combust. I'm gone, free falling into the chasm of my release, screaming incoherently from the sheer intensity of my orgasm. I hear him grunt out my name as he slams into me, forcing me to yet another peak.

We're both breathing heavily when he eventually rolls off of me, landing on his back beside me. My hands land on my stomach, and instead of the post-sex intimacy glow I want, I'm filled with confusion and trepidation. I know how earth-shatteringly amazing that was for me physically, but emotionally I'm a jumbled-up mess. And I have absolutely no clue what Jackson is thinking right now.

"Well, damn." His voice is hoarse but holds a note of pure satisfaction.

I look over to see one arm stretched over his head, putting his muscular torso on display, with a light sheen of sweat covering every inch of his skin. I have to mentally hold myself back from turning on my side and cuddling up against him. I want to. So badly. But just because we had sex doesn't mean things are changing. I don't want them to change.

Do I?

# Chapter Twelve

*Jackson*

I've had more sex with Mila in the last two weeks than I did with Stefani in the last two years of our relationship.

And if that isn't an eye-opener about the true state of my previous relationship, I don't know what is.

That first night was amazing, but there was definitely a strange vibe between us immediately after. I was about to pull her into my arms when she suddenly jumped up out of bed and announced she was taking a shower. I debated joining her for about a second, but when she closed the bathroom door, I got the message. She needed space. I didn't really blame her, I was definitely overwhelmed by the intensity of our connection.

Thankfully, by the time she came out of the bathroom, whatever awkwardness she was feeling had gone. Mila found me sitting in her living room, dressed in my shorts, hanging out with Milo. She walked over, leaned down to kiss me, then asked if I wanted breakfast as if nothing had happened. It was oddly domestic and comfortable. And when I went to kiss her goodbye, she's the one who initiated round two with her hot little hands sliding down the front of my shorts.

Every time has been hotter than the last, and there hasn't been any more awkward vibes. We've settled into this new friends with benefits phase easily, and for the most part I've managed to ignore the gnawing sensation in my gut that's trying to tell me this is more than just friendship.

Every time we go out, it feels easy and natural. I have to remind myself it's not real, that it's all for show. Because kissing the top of her head, wrapping my arms around her, holding her hand — it all feels right. She claims to want nothing more from me than friendship and sex, and of course, our ongoing pretense of a deeper relationship. Which means I'm living the stereotypical douchebag man's fantasy of no-strings-attached sex with a beautiful woman. The benefit is it's someone who I truly enjoy being with. And not just regular sex; it's spectacular, can't stop thinking about it, world-shifting sex. We can't keep our hands off of each other, we're together almost every night. Even our pets get along, with Harley keeping Milo in line any time the big dog is over at my house.

So why the fuck do I feel so unsettled and confused?

I can't seem to stop comparing Mila to my ex, even though the comparison is in no way fair. Don't get me wrong, Mila wins, hands down, in every single way. But associating her with Stefani feels cruel. There is no contest. Being with a woman like Mila, even just as friends with benefits, is showing me how dysfunctional my previous relationship was, and just how wrong for me Stefani really was. At the time, I somehow overlooked the fact that she was always whining about us going out with her friends to fancy bars and restaurants that had overpriced drinks and food far more complicated than it needed to be. You can keep your freeze-dried flower garnishes and seventy dollar bottles of wine, thank you very much. If an invite came from my friends to meet at the bar for a drink, or at a park for a game of frisbee, there was always an excuse for why we couldn't go.

The changes were gradual, I can see that now, but somehow Stefani managed to get her way on just about everything. The apartment we rented was decorated in her style — minimalist, stark white, and expensive-looking. She hated Harley, even if she never admitted it to my face, I knew she did. She wouldn't ever pet him, and I saw the looks of disdain she would give him, even if she didn't realize I saw them. More than once she suggested we get rid of him, but since she always managed to make it sound like she was teasing, I didn't think anything of it. Now I wonder just how serious she had been.

In contrast, Mila is warmth and sunshine, happiness and friendliness. She's down-to-earth and loves animals as much as I do.

Basically, she would be the perfect woman for me. If I had any interest in a real relationship.

When my phone rings with a call from my mom, I check that I've got time to talk with her before work. Mom is chatty, and it has been a while since we talked. Which means I'm in for a long conversation about all of the useless gossip that I don't particularly care about, but I'll pretend to for her sake.

"Hey, Mom."

Her warm voice comes down the line, bringing a smile to my face. "Hi, honey. How are you?"

"I'm doing great. Really happy here. I can't wait for you and Dad to visit." I move around my house, getting everything ready that I'll need at the clinic today.

"Oh, me too. I'm trying to convince your father that we should come next month. But of course, he's more worried about scheduling it around his golf games. I swear, those clubs were the worst retirement present ever. I never see him anymore, and heaven help me if I need help around the house."

Mom's grousing is only halfway serious. I happen to know she secretly loves that my father found a hobby after retiring from his job as an engineer. Their marriage is what marriages should be. Built on trust and love, and most of all, a deep friendship. But after forty years together, having my dad at home all the time started to drive Mom nuts really quickly.

"Tell him there are some great courses over here we can check out. Maybe that will help."

"I'll do that, honey." Mom goes silent.

"What's up, Mom, no gossip to fill me in on?" I tease, but the distressed noise she makes stops me in my tracks. "Mom?"

"Honey, I don't know how to tell you this. I ran into Louanne the other day."

The very mention of Stefani's mom makes my stomach plummet.

"Stefani's pregnant."

I digest this information, letting the news sink in slowly. My ex, the woman I thought I would marry, is pregnant. I don't want her back, and I certainly don't want to have a child with her. Still, finding out she moved on quickly enough to already be pregnant hurts a little. But fast on the heels of that dagger to my self-esteem comes a thought that gives me even more panic.

What if it's mine? Would she go that far?

The next words out of my mother's mouth are both a relief, and a source of even more pain and anger.

"There's more, Jackson. She's due in September."

The math doesn't take me long. "You're fucking joking." I bite out the words, without any remorse for swearing on the phone with my mother. "That would mean she was pregnant before we broke up. Are you sure?"

I don't want to believe it. She might have lied to me about not wanting kids, but surely Stefani didn't cheat on me as well. That would mean...I don't know what that would mean. I already felt betrayed by her, but this is so much worse.

"Honey, I'm so sorry. I didn't want you to hear it from anyone else. I hate that woman for what she did to you."

"Mom, thanks for telling me, but I gotta go."

I hang up the phone without waiting to hear what my mother says. I have to be at the clinic in less than an hour which means it is time to compartmentalize. I can figure out how to handle this insanity after I deal with the animals of Dogwood Cove for the next eight hours.

By some miracle, work is simple enough that it distracts my mind without taking up too much brainpower. Veronica leaves me alone, all of the cases are straightforward and successful, and I even manage to finish my paperwork early. But when I leave the clinic, I don't want to go home. I find myself wandering down the street to Hastings, the bar where I played pool with Mila. Okay, so I didn't go there just to play pool with Mila, but that's what I associate the place with. Come to think of it, I associate most places in town with things I've done with Mila. The pizza joint we've ordered from twice. The beach where we met for a paddle — me on my board, her in her kayak. And of course, The Nutty Muffin, where that woman manages to get me to try every weird and wonderful pastry she creates. She has yet to disappoint.

When I push open the door to the bar, my eyes cast around the dim room. There's no point in denying who I'm looking for, but she isn't here. I do see someone with long blonde hair, instantly reminding me of the fucking insane bomb that my mom dropped on me earlier.

*Stefani cheated on me.*

She's pregnant with someone else's kid. Someone she was with *while* she was with me.

The blonde turns around, and it's Mila's friend Serena. She gives me a wave, I nod back, hoping she doesn't try to come over. I'm not in the mood for small talk. I sit down at the bar and order a double shot of whiskey. I toss it back, and signal for another. That one I take more slowly, and finally I let my mind stew on the news my mom gave me. I honestly thought I was moving on, was over Stefani and what she did. It's been seven months. But the truth is, even though she lied to me about wanting kids, I still loved her when I left. Even knowing we would never work out, I still loved the woman I thought she was. She wasn't perfect, *we* weren't perfect. But at some point, we were good together. And I guess I never really let myself feel the loss of what could have been.

Now any positive feelings I might have held onto about Stefani are blacked out by anger and hurt. My teeth are clenched so tightly my jaw is starting to ache. The roiling in my gut isn't from the whiskey, rather it's from her.

I finish the second glass of whiskey, and the bartender, Dean, I think Mila said was his name, gestures to ask if I want another. I shake my head, pull out some bills from my wallet, and slap them down on the bar top.

The evening air has cooled off by the time I get outside. I'm drunk enough to know I need to be careful walking home, so as not to give the wrong impression to the good folks of Dogwood Cove. I'm also drunk enough to make one really bad decision when I get home.

I dial her number from memory, because deleting it from my phone didn't erase it from my mind.

"Jackson? Why are you calling me?"

She sounds nervous. As she should.

"Got what you really wanted, huh Stef?"

"You're drunk."

I snort. "No shit. Want to know why I'm drunk on a Thursday night? Because my mom had to call me and tell me you're pregnant."

There's a long pause, and even in my current state I know she's trying to figure out how to handle this. I don't give her the chance to come up with any sort of excuse.

"I might not want kids, but even I know how long a woman's pregnancy is, Stefani. Who were you fucking while we were *engaged?*"

"What are you mad about, Jackson? The fact that I'm pregnant or that it isn't yours?" Her voice is mocking me, and I snap. I leap up off the couch, disturbing Harley who was curled up on my lap. I start to pace the small living room.

"Seriously? You think I'm angry that I'm not the father of your child? For fuck's sake, Stef, I didn't want kids. Not with you, not with anyone. Why can't you accept that?" I'm yelling now, and part of me knows I shouldn't, but I can't help it. "What I'm angry about, what fucking *kills* me, is that you cheated. You cheated on me, on our relationship, on the promise we made to each other when you put on a fucking diamond ring and agreed to marry me. *That* is what I'm angry about."

My voice breaks at the end, and I sink down the wall to the floor. I can hear Stefani crying on the other end of the phone, and a small, stupid part of me still hates that I upset her. She deserves to know how I feel, however. She deserves to feel a small part of the pain she caused me.

"I'm sorry, Jackson. Honestly, I am. I never meant for it to happen. I was going to break up with you earlier, but it was so hard to walk away from what we had. Then when I found out I was pregnant, I knew I had to. I didn't want to hurt you, I swear."

"How the hell am I meant to believe any word you say?"

"Jackson..."

Her sobbing just makes me shake my head. "Goodbye Stefani. Good luck with whoever the guy is that was good enough for you to cheat on me. I hope you're happy. I am. Without you."

I hang up and toss my phone across the room before dropping my head into my hands. I thought confronting her would make me feel better, give me some closure. Instead, I feel like shit. I feel like someone took my heart that was finally starting to heal, ripped it out of my chest, and stomped on it. Infidelity is the ultimate betrayal. How the hell do I move on from this, how do I ever let someone in again?

My mind goes to Mila.

No. I can't think about her right now.

I stand up and go to the kitchen, pulling out the bottle of tequila that I brought back from Mexico two years ago. It was my first vacation with Stefani after we had moved in together. I could dump the shit down the drain and smash the bottle, but why waste good liquor. I pop the bottle open, pour a shot and slam it down, wincing as it burns my throat. But I don't stop, drinking another shot, and then another.

Now the room is swimming. Maybe three shots was too many after the double whiskeys earlier. But I feel numb. Numb is good.

Somehow, I make my way into my bedroom, and manage to remove my shirt and pants before I fall down onto my bed face first.

The last thought that crosses my mind before the tequila-soaked oblivion takes over is clear.

I'm better off alone. That way, no one else can hurt me.

# Chapter Thirteen

*Mila*

I looked up *ghosted* in an online urban dictionary last night. It might as well have had a picture of Jackson underneath the definition.

After two weeks of being together every damn day and night, and having sex on every surface in both of our houses, he has disappeared.

He hasn't been in to the bakery the last two mornings. Two days without a muffin, not even the disgusting geriatric bran that he prefers. I'm worried. That's okay, right? Friends can worry about each other. I'm not being too clingy by wanting to see him, or by wondering what the heck is going on. But every time I picked up my phone to type out a message, I stop myself. This isn't a real relationship, which means I don't really have any right to him or his time. Except, I do in a way. Yesterday Paige asked if Jackson would be coming to Summer's barbecue at the resort next week and I didn't know how to answer her. Then, just this afternoon, I ran into Sharon Morton at the grocery store, and she mentioned how much she was looking forward to having Jackson and I over for dinner, and was there a night that worked best for my schedule? Again, I was left clueless on how to answer.

When I leave the store, I go to my Jeep and open my phone. Time to end the radio silence.

> **MILA: Hey, are you okay? Haven't seen you around lately. Also, what's the deal with dinner at the Mortons? Let me know if you need your pretend girlfriend, or whatever.**

I hit send before I can overthink my message, even though re-reading it kind of makes me cringe. *Or whatever*? What the heck does that even mean? Good job, Mila. Way to communicate clearly.

I wait for a few minutes, staring at my phone, willing it to vibrate with a response. When it doesn't, I decide to throw caution to the wind and go find the man in question. Nothing like a little confrontation to help things along.

I drive to the vet clinic, without any sort of plan for how to explain my presence there. Then again, if I'm "dating" the vet, why do I need an excuse to visit him? Firm in my resolve, I pull open the door to the clinic. I smile at Lenora Wong, who's sitting in the waiting room. She always orders cranberry orange scones for her Saturday brunch club.

I walk up to the front desk and am about to ask Rosie if Jackson is in when Veronica pushes through the door to the back. As soon as she sees me, her hand goes to her hip and she sneers at me.

Bad idea, bitch. Today is not the day to pick a fight with me. I ignore her, and focus on Rosie, behind the front desk.

"Hi, Rosie. Can I talk to —"

"This is a *professional* establishment, Mila. We don't need you coming in here acting all inappropriate again." Her nasally voice interrupts me. I'm pretty sure that if my eyebrows went any higher, they would be on top of my head.

"Gee, Veronica, thanks for that reminder. I would hate to be unprofessional and, you know, visit my boyfriend at work." She doesn't miss the emphasis I put on the word boyfriend, if the narrowing of her eyes is any indication. Instead, she pushes past me, and pastes on a large smile to take Mrs. Wong and her cat into the examination room.

"Bitch," I mutter under my breath, but clearly I'm not quiet enough because I hear a soft giggle and realize Rosie heard me. "Sorry, Rosie, that was rude. Is Jackson here?"

The older woman waves me off and shakes her head. "Oh, don't worry, Veronica needed to be cut down a peg or two. The way she went after Jackson before the two of you were together was shameful. But he isn't here today, dear. He switched with Doctor Morton, and has the day off." She frowns in confusion. "I'm surprised he didn't tell you."

I scramble to come up with a believable lie. Fuck, I hate this. "Oh, you're right, how silly of me. I completely forgot. He must be down at the beach. Thanks, Rosie!" I turn and hurry out of the clinic, cheeks burning with embarrassment. Goddamnit, Jackson Holt, where are you and what the *hell* is going on?

I decide to head home and drop off my groceries before going to find him anywhere else. On my way home, I drive past his house and see his car is missing. Yeah, he must be at the beach. He told me once that the water is his happy place. If he's upset about something, that's where he'll be. And no, I'm not going to dwell on the fact that I know him well enough to know this.

Groceries unloaded, I grab Milo's leash and we get back in the Jeep. Since I have to go past the bakery, I decide to stop in and pick up some goodies. Maybe I can get him to open up about what's going on with food.

Riley and her husband Dean are inside when I get to The Nutty Muffin, and she waves me over with a smile.

"Hey, guys." I lead Milo over and sit down next to Riley's wheelchair. She reaches down and pets Milo, who has rested his head in her lap, while Dean gives me a concerned frown.

"Is Jackson feeling better?"

"Umm, yes?" It comes out sounding more like a question than a statement, but as is very apparent today, I have no idea what's going on with my alleged boyfriend.

"That's good. He seemed pretty upset the other night when he came into Hastings. Never saw a guy pound two double whiskeys so fast."

"Oh. Right, ah, yeah he's fine now. Just got some news that upset him. I'm actually on my way to find him right now."

Riley looks up from Milo and touches my arm. "Is everything okay between you two?"

I jump up. "Yup, fine. Just gonna grab some cookies and go to meet him. See you later." I hurry over to the counter and load up a bag with some cookies. When I turn to head out again, Riley is parked in front of me with her arms crossed.

"Out with it, Monroe."

Fuck. I should have known my lies would catch up to me eventually. Honestly? I need to talk to someone. Tell the truth, and ask if I'm going insane or not. Riley doesn't know it, but she just volunteered.

"Okay, but not here. Follow me." I lead Riley through the kitchen and out the back door. When I've made sure we're alone, I start to pace. The pent-up energy from keeping everything a secret, and from not knowing what's wrong with Jackson has built to the point of exploding.

"Jackson and I aren't really dating. We're fake dating. We need everyone to think it's real, but it isn't. But I think I like him. *Really* like him, not *fake* like him. I can't do anything about it, though, and he's pulling away, and I don't know why, and I'm pretty sure I'm nuts. Oh, and no one knows except you, so please don't tell anyone."

Riley stares at me, openmouthed, for several seconds. "Umm, wow. That's...definitely not what I was expecting. Okay. There's a lot to unpack here." She turns her wheelchair from side to side absently. "So the whole relationship is pretend."

I give her a weary nod and sink down into the folding chair that we keep out here for breaks. "Yeah. He needed to convince Doctor Morton that he was committed to staying here, and I needed to get my family and friends off my back about working too much."

"Huh, okay. I mean, I guess it makes sense, but damn girl. What a mess."

My head falls back against the cement wall with a thunk. "Tell me about it."

The door to the kitchen opens, and Kelly pokes her head outside. "Sorry to interrupt, but Riley, Dean is looking for you."

I stand up. "I should go and find Jackson anyway."

Riley wheels toward the door, stops, and turns to face me. "Be careful, Mila. This seems like you're setting yourself up for nothing but trouble."

"Trust me, I know. But I don't have a choice now."

She eyes me thoughtfully. "You could always tell the truth. To Jackson, and to everyone else."

I shake my head vehemently. "No. Can't do that."

Riley shrugs, and wheels through the bakery, back to her loving husband. I watch her go, and an unfamiliar feeling of envy weaves through me. I want that. I shake my head quickly. No time to dwell on that kind of fantasy; I've got a pretend boyfriend to find and grill.

I speed the entire way through town to the public beach. Sure enough, Jackson's car is parked up at the far end, away from the crowded area by the playground. I park next to him, grab Milo and the bag of cookies, and head down to the water. I see him paddling far out from shore and decide to wait. He's not getting away without talking to me.

I unclip Milo's leash, and he instantly starts snuffling around until he finds a stick, which he drops at my feet expectantly. I take off my shoes and wander down to the water's edge, and throw the stick out as far as I can, watching Milo swim out to get it. Keeping one eye on my dog, I glance over to Jackson. He's turned toward me now, and there's no way he hasn't seen me. Slowly he paddles closer, until he's near enough for Milo to realize it's him. The dog drops the stick and instantly starts to swim closer to Jackson, and over the water I hear his laughter when Milo tries to climb up on the board. Whatever is wrong, it can't be that bad if he can still laugh at my dog's antics. Jackson drops down to his knees and helps Milo up. I can't help but giggle at the sight of the giant mutt standing at the front of Jackson's paddle board while he tries to get them both to shore. Eventually they reach me, Milo jumping off, almost upsetting Jackson into the water before going off in search for another stick.

"Hi," I say, sliding my hands into the back pockets of my shorts to stop myself from reaching out to him.

"Hey, Mila," he answers, so quietly I barely hear him. He picks up his board and walks out of the water, with a brief backward glance to make sure I follow. We reach a log where I see his towel and bag. He pulls out a T-shirt, and puts it on before sitting down on the log and looking up at me expectantly.

"You found me, so what's up?"

"What's up? Umm, how about, where did you go this week?" I instantly want to take back the words as soon as I say them, hating how needy and clingy they sound. "I just meant it was weird to not see you, and I didn't know what to say when people were asking about you. If you want to cut back on our arrangement that's fine, I just would like to know."

"Sorry. I know I should have talked to you. I just...Fuck." He drops his head down to his chest, his hands coming up to the back of his neck.

I want to go to him, sit beside him and wrap my arms around him. But something is nagging at me, telling me things are about to change. So I don't. I stand there and wait for the axe to fall.

"I just think we should go back to friends and fake dating, that's all."

I nod slowly, trying to understand. "No more sex."

"Exactly. It's not that I didn't enjoy it." For the first time, I see a glint of something in his eyes, but it's gone in a flash. "But I worry that sex will lead to feelings, and things will get messy between us. And we both don't want messy."

"Right. Messy would be bad." I chew on the inside of my cheek, trying to figure out how to ask what I need to ask. "So can I just ask, why the change? I thought things were just fine." That's not true. They weren't fine, because every time we came together, I fell for him a little more. He's right, it did get messy. But stopping now won't fix that.

Jackson stands up and walks down to the water, letting the gentle waves cover his feet. I follow him, because what else can I do. Pain and anger are radiating off him in waves.

"My ex is pregnant. She's due in two months. If you do the math, that means she got pregnant while we were still engaged. And here's the kicker, the kid isn't mine." He barks out a harsh laugh. "I thought it hurt finding out she had lied to me for years about wanting kids. But newsflash, finding out she was fucking someone else behind my back hurts even more."

"Oh, Jackson," I murmur, my hand reaching out to touch his shoulder. But he flinches and pulls away, and I drop it back to my side, trying to ignore the sting of his rejection. "I'm so sorry she did that to you, and I wish I could find her and slap her for being such a bitch. But I'm not her, and what we're doing isn't the same. Our friendship has always been about honesty and trust, hasn't it?"

He turns to me, a desperate and wild glint in his eyes. "Exactly. And that friendship is important to me, Mila. It means so much. I can't risk it, can't risk losing your friendship by confusing things anymore than we already are by lying to everyone else."

"So you want to end that, too?"

Jackson winces, and looks guilty when he responds. "No, not yet, unless you want to." I quickly shake my head. "Morton is close to offering me partnership, that's why he wants us over for dinner, I think. If we can keep it up for a little longer..."

"Yeah. Of course. A deal is a deal. You've managed to get my friends and my brother to back off and leave me alone about being a workaholic, so now I get to help secure you that job." The words sound hollow to me, but I know it's what he wants to hear.

"Right. But the rest of it," he pauses, and I finish for him.

"The rest of it ends."

It has been a couple of days since I confronted Jackson at the beach about his disappearing act, and I'd like to say things have gone back to normal, except I don't really know what normal is for us. He has come into the bakery each morning, given me a brief kiss, picked up his coffee and muffin and left, claiming he needs to get to the clinic. It's as if he's doing just enough to maintain pretenses and nothing more.

Tonight we're expected at the Morton's house for dinner, and I can't help but wonder how awkward this is going to be. It's obvious he's still having a hard time being around me, much less being affectionate toward me, but this is the ultimate test. If tonight goes well, Morton will probably offer him the partnership, and the weeks of lying to our friends will have been worth it. And we can start to plan the demise of our fake relationship.

In some sick and twisted way, I don't want it to end. I hate lying, but I don't hate being around Jackson. I definitely don't hate holding his hand or kissing him; in fact, I miss both of those things. When he said we needed to stop having sex, I had to hide my disappointment. Not only because the sex was so damn good, but because the connection I felt with him was so powerful. I guess I had fooled myself into thinking that maybe it could become something real. Something with feelings involved.

Except feelings get messy.

When he picks me up, I have to check the corner of my mouth for drool. Goddamnit, it should be illegal to look that good in a button up shirt and khakis.

"You look beautiful," he says quietly, his eyes traveling down my body. Even if our relationship is strictly *just friends* now, I still took the time to put on a fancy set of lingerie underneath my dress. Even if he doesn't see it, I feel good, and that's what matters right now.

"Thanks. Shall we?" I dodge his hand, needing to avoid physical contact as long as possible in an act of self-preservation. The brief kisses I get in the morning are hard enough to take without wanting more. Tonight is the first time we've had to really pretend to be together in almost a week, and I'm nervous.

When we get to Doctor Morton's large house, Jackson comes around and opens my door for me. I step out, and he moves to take my hand, pausing before he touches me. "Is this okay?" he murmurs.

I give a quick nod and take his hand, ignoring the jolt of electricity that runs through me. His hand is warm and solid. Strong, just like he is. And I'm hit with flashes of memories of his hands running all over my body.

No. Stop. Abort. Must not think about sex with the man I can't have sex with anymore, especially not in front of his boss.

Sharon Morton opens the door, and I can see Doctor Morton standing behind her with a welcoming smile on his face.

"Mila, Jackson, we're so glad you're here."

It's showtime.

# Chapter Fourteen



Sitting next to Mila, touching her, pretending to be with her, in front of my boss no less, is a special kind of fucking torture. Seeing her in that dress when I picked her up, all I wanted to do was push her inside, close the door, and strip her naked to feast on her. Holding her hand as we walked up to the house was like latching onto an anchor in a storm. But I can't shake the ghost of Stefani's betrayal. No matter how much I want to believe Mila is different, that a real relationship with her would be different, I'm not there yet.

When Phil invites me out to the patio for a beer while he checks the grill, I go gladly. A few minutes away from her intoxicating perfume will hopefully let me get myself back under control. I clearly underestimated how hard it would be to go back to just being friends with her.

I keep reminding myself that we just have to get through this dinner, and a few more dates; whatever it takes to convince Phil

I'm here to stay. Then we can part as friends. And all I need to do is make damn sure I don't let myself fall for Mila Monroe.

"Mila's a lovely woman." Phil makes the comment sound like a casual observation, but I've learned there's more to what he says.

"She is."

"You're a good fit for this town, Jackson. I hope you feel the same way." He turns and looks at me, his beer in one hand. Phil Morton is a good man, a good boss, and he would be a good business partner. I know that all of these hoops I've been jumping through are only because he wants the best for his practice and for the town. I can understand the need to prove myself before he just hands over half of his business, even if I do think my dating Mila as the deciding factor is a bit ridiculous.

"I do, Phil. I'm really happy here; Dogwood Cove is exactly the kind of place I see myself staying for a good long time."

"Maybe starting a family some day?" he asks, and I wince. This is one thing I won't lie about.

"You know, a family isn't really in the cards for me." I take a sip of my own beer, debating how much to share. I guess if we're going to be business partners, we're going to get personal. "I've never wanted kids. A wife, absolutely. But no children."

If Phil is surprised by my revelation, he hides it well. "I see, well, I can respect that. It was expected of my generation to have a family, but these days things are different. How does Mila feel about that?"

"With respect, Phil, her thoughts on children are not mine to share."

Phil claps his hand on my shoulder. "Good point. No need to gossip. Now, these steaks look perfect. Shall we eat?"

I follow him inside, breathing an internal sigh of relief that things went as well as could be expected with that conversation. When we get inside and I see Mila smiling with Sharon Morton over the salad bowl she's mixing, I realize something. Dogwood Cove *is* a town I can see myself living in for a long time, because of her.

Which makes me wonder how I'll feel when she and I are no longer pretending to be together.

We make it through dinner. My arm is draped over the back of Mila's chair at times, and my fingers skate across her bare shoulders. I notice every little thing she does, as if my senses are hyperaware of her. The way she shifts in her seat, leaning toward me, the elegant line of her neck when she swallows a sip of her wine, the light laugh she gives to Phil's jokes. When her hand lands on my leg at one point, she snatches it away as if she forgot our decision to go back to just friends. I want to grab her hand and put it back, but I don't. I set this boundary, so I need to maintain it. Even if that fleeting touch of her hand seared me to my soul.

Later on, when I drop her off at her house, I walk beside her up to the front door.

"Thank you for doing this tonight," I say, putting my hands in my pockets. Mila peers up at me, and her smile doesn't reach her eyes. I wish it did.

"Of course. Do you think it worked? Will he offer you partnership?"

"Yeah, I think it's coming. I understand he wants to make sure I'm serious about the job and about staying here, and I think he sees that now."

Mila fidgets with the keys in her hands. "You don't think when we break up, he'll change his mind?"

I shake my head firmly. "No. The job isn't contingent on me being in a relationship. Phil might have some old-fashioned ideas but he isn't that conservative. He'll probably give me hell for letting you go, though."

That makes her chuckle softly under her breath, and I can't help it. I tip her chin up so her eyes meet mine. "Besides, we'll stay friends, no matter what."

"Friends."

She says it so softly I almost don't hear her. I wonder if the word leaves a bitter taste in her mouth like it does for me.

"Okay. Well, goodnight." I drop my hand and take a step back, waiting as she unlocks her door. But just as she's about to step through, I move. "Wait." I close the short distance between us, cup her face in my hands, and kiss her. She melts into me, our lips coming together like they were made for this. I force myself to keep it brief, to not consume her the way the unbroken part of me wants to. Seeing her face flushed with desire when I pull back almost makes me change my mind, but self-preservation wins out.

"Just in case the neighbors were watching." The words fall flat as soon as they leave my mouth and I wish I could rewind ten seconds and not say them. I cheapened our kiss, our connection, and made it all about the show.

It *is* all for show.

Because I made it that way.

"Goodnight, Jackson." Mila whirls around and slips through her door, closing it and locking it behind her. I'm left standing on her porch, wondering when it all went wrong. I know I've made a huge mistake somewhere along the way. The question is, was it agreeing to fake date her, sleeping with her, or is it right now — standing here and not admitting to myself that I'm falling for her?

My phone wakes me up early the next morning from an unfamiliar number. I answer it groggily, to hear Ethan Monroe's deep voice in my ear.

"Sorry to wake you, man; I figured you got up with Mila. Not that I want to think about you and my sister in bed. Fuck," he grinds out the curse, and I let out a low laugh.

"No worries. What can I do for you?"

"I'm working on the bakery expansion today and could use an extra set of hands at some point. Reid's busy getting the school ready for September, so Summer suggested I ask you." His voice gets even more gruff as he continues. "She thinks we should be friends since you're dating my sister. And yes, I know that sounds pansy-ass stupid, but don't tell her I said that."

I sit up in bed, trying not to think about how fucking odd it is to be on the phone with my fake girlfriend's brother, while wearing nothing but my boxers.

"Yeah, I can do that. I have to be at the clinic after lunch, though."

"That's fine. Come on down whenever, we should be done with what I need help on by then."

Half an hour later I push open the door to the space next to The Nutty Muffin. Ethan is hunched over a table looking at some plans, but he glances my way and gives me a wave.

"Coffee and muffins from next door are over there, help yourself."

I walk over and pour a mug of coffee and take a bite of a carrot muffin. Goddamn, Mila can bake. Somehow, when our pretend relationship is over, I need to find a way to keep visiting the bakery for coffee and muffins. We might have agreed to remain friends, but something tells me that will be easier said than done.

"So what are we working on?" I ask, coming to stand beside Ethan.

"Most of it I can do myself, but I need to lift this beam up," he points to a long, thick, square piece of wood on the floor, "and it'll be a team effort. Mila and Summer are going to come over when we go to lift, but first we've got some prep work. Have you done any renovations before?"

I shake my head, "No, can't say that I have. But I know which end of the hammer to hold, if that helps."

Ethan chuckles at that. "Yeah, that's fine. I'll give you the simple jobs."

I quickly finish my coffee and muffin. Ethan hands me a tool belt, and points me in the direction of some bracing that needs to be in place before we can install the beam. For a while we work in a companionable silence; the repetitive motion of hammering nails is soothing in a weird way.

"I know it might not seem this way, but I'm glad you and Mila hooked up."

Ethan's statement comes out of nowhere and I almost drop the hammer I'm holding. "Okay," I say warily.

"She needs someone who makes her realize there's more to life than just the bakery. The girls get her out for yoga and book club, but my sister is obsessed with this place. You can help her find balance." He puts down the board he was cutting and comes closer, crossing his arms over his chest. I'm not a small guy, but Ethan has this gruff, large presence that makes me stand up even taller. "Do you know why this expansion is so important to her?"

I shake my head.

"She opened the bakery two years before our parents died. Mom taught her how to bake, taught her everything she knows. And it was Mom's dream to open a café in town. They used to talk about turning the bakery into something more, a place that served lunch and not just baked goods, but Mila always refused to let Mom and Dad invest in her or pay for anything. She said she had to do it herself or it wouldn't feel right. I think she regrets that decision now. If she had joined forces with Mom, they could have opened the café together. Now she wants to do it in Mom's memory. The problem is, she's been so focused on making enough money to be able to do this on her own that she's forgotten to live her own damn life." He looks down at the floor, then back up at me, and there's a fire in his eyes I haven't seen before. "She's got other reasons for hesitating with relationships. I don't know details, but I know enough. Which is why I need to say one more thing. Hurt her, and you'll have me to answer to."

My eyes widen, and I manage to croak out, "Got it." Ethan nods and turns back to work, leaving me to my thoughts. I think about how busy Mila is, between the rental properties she and Ethan own, and the bakery, and I understand what he is — and is not — saying. She has buried herself in work, heading toward a goal she can't let go of. A goal she will do anything to achieve. I know the feeling.

"Hey, handsome," Summer's voice comes in, and I look over to see Mila following behind. Her dark hair is swept back in a braid, but a few pieces have come out. As she walks over to me,

I see a smudge of something on her cheek, and when she stands beside me, my thumb comes out to sweep it off.

"Thanks," she murmurs, looking up at me through her long lashes.

I bend down and give her a kiss. "The muffins were delicious."

"Okay, you two, enough canoodling. Let's get building."

Mila looks over at Summer and arches her brow. "Canoodling? What are we, seventy? Besides, if anyone is guilty of too much PDA, it's you."

I watch with a smirk as Summer wraps her arms around Ethan's waist and leans her head against his chest. Mila rolls her eyes, but her hand seeks out mine.

"I can't help it if your brother is irresistible."

"Enough already. Shorty, I love you, but stop harassing my sister. Mila, I'm happy you're happy but I don't need to see it. Got it?" Ethan's tone is teasing, but I see the way he looks at the girls. One is his sister, and one is his soulmate. He's a lucky guy.

We get to work, following Ethan's directions, and soon the beam is hoisted into the air and settled on the supports I helped to build. When we're done, the four of us stand back and look at it.

"That's a good-looking beam," Mila says, clasping her hands under her chin. She looks so adorably excited; I don't think twice before wrapping my arms around her and tugging her back into my chest. She tips her head up and looks at me curiously, but I just hold her. I can tell myself it's just to make sure we're convincing in front of Summer and Ethan, but the truth is, the more time I spend with Mila, the more time I *want* to spend with her. And when I'm with her, it's getting harder and harder to keep my hands to myself.

So what am I going to do when I no longer have the excuse of our fake relationship to fall back on? When I can't touch her or kiss her and justify it as playing a role?

# Chapter Fifteen

*Mila*

I'm taking a rare Saturday morning off with the girls to hit the Westport Farmers Market. I didn't want to, but it's hard to say no when Summer, Serena, *and* Paige are all ganging up on me. They didn't really give me much of a choice when they arranged for Kelly to deal with all of the baking and Sebastian to run the front of house. Those two really will make good managers when I'm ready to take that step.

As I walk arm in arm with Serena down the colourful stalls of the market, I have to admit it was a good idea. Getting out of the bakery, out of Dogwood Cove, and out of Jackson's powerful orbit is making me breathe a deep sigh of relief. It's hard to be around him right now. I've had a taste of something more from him, even if, for him, it was just physical. Going back to a friendship, with our forced PDA's only when absolutely necessary, is hard.

The worst part is, I'm so in tune with everything he does that every now and then I catch a glance or I sense a vibe coming from him that makes me wonder if he's struggling with our re-established boundaries as much as I am.

Not that it matters. After our dinner at the Morton's house, I went home and promised myself I wouldn't be the one to change the rules.

"All I'm saying is, Finn seems really nice. Ask Mila, rumour has it she dated him years ago."

Summer's voice penetrates my thoughts and I try to catch up on what they're talking about.

"I'm not going to be sloppy seconds to Mila," Serena replies indignantly, squeezing my arm tightly. "You can't come after a ten like her and expect to measure up."

I scoff at that. "Oh, please. Serena, you're a twelve with your dancer body and long blonde hair. Besides, Finn and I dated for like, a month, years ago. Guaranteed you wouldn't be second. That man goes through women like I go through bags of flour at the bakery. A new one every week."

"Are you talking about me, Mila Monroe?"

I instantly blush as Finn McNeil, one of my brother's good friends, comes up beside me.

"Hello, ladies, looking lovely today."

If it were possible to have a degree in flirting, Finn would be top of the class. He drapes his arm over my shoulder, and our friendship is the only thing preventing me from shoving him away.

"You don't think it's odd that hearing me talk about a man-whore makes you think I must be referring to you?" I poke him in his side.

"I can't help it if I'm irresistible."

"Are you going to help me choose wine for the barbecue or not?" Summer interrupts, taking Finn's arm and dragging us over to the booth he's running. Finn is the new head sommelier at a local winery, and he offered to provide wine for Summer's re-opening barbecue at Oceanside Resort happening next week.

The next half hour is spent sampling wine, eventually settling on a white and a rosé. We leave Finn with his promise to deliver a case of each to the resort for the barbecue, and make our way to the food trucks lined up on the edge of the market. Once the four of us have our lunches, we find an empty picnic table and sit down to eat.

"Things looked pretty cozy between you and Jackson the other day," Summer comments casually, smiling at me over her salad.

"Mmhmm," I mumble, quickly taking a large bite of my grilled brie and fig jam sandwich, hoping to avoid having to answer.

"Ooh, yes, c'mon Mila, we haven't heard *anything*." Serena waggles her eyebrows at me. "You never let Summer tell us about her sex life, so you *have* to share yours!"

"That's because Summer is dating Mila's brother and it would be incredibly uncomfortable for her to hear about his sexual encounters," Paige chimes in, before turning toward me and adjusting her tortoiseshell rimmed glasses. "But given how lackluster the intimacy has been in this month's book club pick, I think we would all appreciate a salacious story or two."

"Enough with the big words, Paigey," Serena nudges Paige before clapping her hands together. "Now. Out with it, Mila."

I can feel the heat on my face and I know that I'm blushing. But all three of them are looking at me expectantly. "The sex is great." It is. Or, it was.

"And..." Summer gestures at me.

"And." I shrug. "I don't know, guys, this is weird. It's really great."

Serena throws up her hands. "You're hopeless."

Paige takes pity on me and stands up from the table. "Come on, we can't force her to talk. Not without alcohol."

"Then let's go back to Finn and get a bottle or two."

"You're ridiculous," I say, standing up with Paige. "Come on, I want to check out the rest of the market."

By no small miracle Serena and Summer drop the subject of my sex life, and we continue on. By the time we leave the market, we're all full of delicious samples, and bags overflowing with produce and artisanal goodies. I forgot how much I love the farmer's market. Years ago, I considered having a stall here to sell my muffins. But when Mom and Dad died, that idea got pushed way down to the bottom of my priority list. Maybe once Mom's café is up and running, I can think about it again.

Thinking about the café makes me think about the other day, watching Jackson help Ethan. It was clear he had no idea what he was doing, but the look of pride when Ethan clapped him on the back and thanked him for his help was endearingly sweet.

Back at my house, I let Milo out into the yard to run around and play, and I open the messaging app on my phone.

**MILA: Want to meet up for a walk with Milo later today?**

**JACKSON: Sure. It's been a few days since we were seen out and about.**

Ouch. That hurts.

**MILA: Right.**

My phone starts to vibrate in my hand with an incoming call from Jackson.

"Mila, I'm sorry. As soon as I hit send, I realized how fucking asshole-ish that sounded." His tone is full of regret and just like that, the sting from his words subsides.

"It's okay. I get it. And you're right, it has been a while," I say.

"Yeah, but I don't only want to see you because of our agreement. I like spending time with you, Mila." His voice grows softer, more tender, and I have to work hard not to read too much into it.

"I...like spending time with you, too."

The line is silent for a few seconds and I wonder if I shouldn't have said that. Are the lines getting blurry between us or is it just me?

"Meet you at the gazebo in half an hour?" His voice sounds husky, and it sends a delicious shiver down my spine. The crappy part is, I don't think he has any clue how much he affects me.

When I see Jackson walking up to Milo and I exactly half an hour later, those shivers intensify. His eyes are warm, and he's smiling when he bends down to kiss me.

"Hi."

He takes my hand as if us walking my dog together is an everyday occurrence, and my brain finally catches up to my heart.

I *want* this to be my every day.

I want *him* to be my every day.

This past week has been a blur of long days and sleepless night. I only wish I was losing sleep for a better reason than agonizing over the fact that somewhere along the way I fell in love with Jackson Holt.

My every waking minute has been occupied with work between the bakery, the expansion, and helping Summer with last minute resort tasks. I should be exhausted, and physically I am. But mentally my stupid brain will not shut off.

I fell in love with a man who will most likely run scared all the way to the next town if I tell him how I feel. The worst part is, everyone knows something is up with me. My friends keep asking me what's wrong, Ethan couldn't possibly frown any deeper when he sees me, and Jackson...well, thinking about him only makes matters worse. So, I've been avoiding him all week — keeping our interactions at the bakery as brief as possible and giving any number of excuses for why I can't see him in the evenings. If he suspects anything, he hasn't said so, and I'm not sure if his obliviousness makes it easier or harder for me.

But today there will be no avoiding anyone. It's the re-opening barbecue at Oceanside Resort that Summer has been planning for months. She wants to host the entire town as a way to say thank you for all of the help and support she's had getting the place up and running again.

Which means Jackson and I need to be extra convincing in our "relationship". He picked me up earlier, looking downright delicious in khaki coloured shorts and a dark blue Henley style T-shirt that is molded to his muscular torso. The top button is undone, showing just a slice of his tanned chest. I have no idea what we talk about, I'm too distracted by his hand holding mine. Why is he holding my hand in the car? No one can see us. It's things like this that are making me feel completely nuts.

When Jackson parks his car at the resort, I go to open my door and he stops me with a hand on my leg.

"Mila, before we go out there, what's going on?"

"What...what do you mean?" I stammer out. I hate that I always feel two steps behind when it comes to Jackson and I. If he pushes me to talk right now, I might just spill the truth about how I feel. And *that* can't happen.

"I haven't seen you all week, and you barely paid attention the entire drive out here." He gives me a wry grin. "Or do you really want to try pickle pizza next week."

"Eww. No," I say immediately. "I'm sorry. I guess I'm...distracted." I glance out the window to where I can see all of our friends hustling with finishing touches.

"By what?"

"What is this, twenty questions?" I fire back.

"I guess that depends on your answers."

That makes me shake my head in resignation. But our banter has given me just enough time to close the lid on my pesky feelings, and remember the boundaries between us. "Sorry. I've just been so busy with the expansion and with helping Summer get ready for today. I'll be fine."

*Please believe me. Please believe me. Please believe me.*

My silent prayer works, because after the briefest of seconds, Jackson nods, and moves his hand from my leg.

"Okay."

I internally sag with relief when he gets out of the car and walks around to open my door. But when he helps me out and pulls me straight into his warm, solid body for a hug, his arms coming around me send all of my senses into overdrive once again.

"You know I'm here for you if you need anything, right?"

"Mmhmm," I mumble into his shirt, breathing deeply. God, he smells so good.

"Mila! Jackson! Hey, guys!" Riley's cheerful voice breaks us apart, and I look over to see Dean lifting her wheelchair out of the back of their car. As I start to head over to say hello, someone else calls Jackson's name from down by the beach.

"It's Phil. Do you mind if I…" he gestures toward the beach.

"No, go, I'll be down in a minute." I say, giving him an encouraging smile.

He bends down and gives me a quick kiss on the cheek and my eyes flutter closed then he's gone.

"Man, you've got it bad."

I open my eyes to see Riley beside me.

"Come on, you've been working here all this time so you can show me the best way to get around."

We leave Dean at their car and set off toward the main building. Summer made sure there was a paved path all the way to the dock and down to the first beachfront cabin, which she decided to make fully accessible after meeting Riley and hearing about how there are few fully accessible vacation spots for people with mobility challenges. We take off toward the pier, where Summer has tables laden with food. At several people's urging, she turned the barbecue into a potluck, so everyone has brought their favourite dishes. My mouth starts to water just thinking about it.

"Does the good doctor know you're hopelessly in love with him?"

The way Riley asks the question so casually makes me trip over my own feet.

"What?"

She pivots her chair to partially block me on the path. Thankfully there's no one around us right now to see the blush that I can feel creeping all over my face.

"You heard me. You're in love with him."

"Riley. Shh." I gesture frantically to try and get her to stop talking. I'm not ready for this. What if Jackson hears her?

"Oh relax. No one is around. So, out with it. Does he know?"

"No. He doesn't. And he can't, because he wants to stay friends, remember?" I fold my arms across my chest defensively.

"I get why you guys started the whole pretend relationship thing. It was smart, at first. But you need to tell him things have changed for you," she says gently. "He deserves to know an amazing woman has fallen for him."

"I —"

Thankfully, I notice Riley's eyes widen almost comically and I stop talking because two arms snake around my waist and I'm pulled back against Jackson's broad chest.

"Hello ladies. Everyone's starting to dish up the food. You should come and get in line."

"Great idea. Oh look, there's Dean." Riley waves at her husband. "Mila. Think about it."

She turns and wheels quickly over to Dean, who's standing in line. He bends down and kisses her, and seeing their real, deep, honest love sends a pang of longing through me. I've never wanted that...until now.

# Chapter Sixteen

*Jackson*

"Thank you, Mrs. Hopkins. I'm sure Mila and I will really enjoy the pie, it was very kind of you to drop it off." I wave at my patient as she leaves the clinic, having dropped off a strawberry rhubarb pie. Apparently, it's Mila's favourite, and Mrs. Hopkins thought I could surprise her with it tonight. The way the old lady winked at me when she suggested a romantic dinner was mildly uncomfortable, but I guess I'm getting used to how over-involved everyone is in each other's lives here. And the pie does look delicious. Too bad I'm not exactly sure when I'll get to share it with my "girlfriend".

Something is up with Mila. And I feel like a total idiot because for the life of me I cannot figure out what it is. She's pulling back, which should be a relief. After all, I'm the one who wants to stay just friends. But ever since the barbecue at Oceanside, I've felt her drifting away. Part of me wishes there were someone I could ask about her to make sure everything is okay. But no one knows the truth of our relationship, and it would be more than a little suspicious for me to ask her brother or one of her friends if they know what is going on with her.

I tried to get her alone at the bakery this morning, but she gave me the smallest smile, accompanied by a faint blush on her cheeks, before darting back into the kitchen. She claimed she had muffins that needed to go in the oven, but it felt more like an excuse to avoid me.

I'm trying to convince myself this is for the best. That creating some space now will make our eventual "breakup" easier. But easier on who? The truth is, I miss her. I miss eating pizza on her back porch, I miss holding her hand while we walk Milo, I miss kissing her over coffee at the bakery.

When I moved to Dogwood Cove I was looking to move on from the rubble of my life in Vancouver. I made the conscious decision to not entertain even the idea of a relationship, not just because my heart was still damaged from my ex, but because I didn't want anything or anyone clouding my thoughts while I focused on my career. Then I met Mila Monroe, and little by little she weaved her way into my life, and my heart.

She's more than just a friend. I'm not fully ready to admit how much more, but I can't deny it anymore, either. The same way I can't deny how easy it was to be with her, even if we were only pretending. She has shown me that the balance I've always sought in life is possible, and it's given me a shred of hope that I don't have to be alone forever.

I've been hitting the beach almost every day, getting in as much paddling as I can before the weather starts to turn colder.

Every time I pull into the parking lot, I scan for Mila's blue Jeep, but I haven't seen her and Milo there in a while. She's definitely avoiding me.

After four days of this, I'm resolved to find her tomorrow and convince her to talk to me. Call it being a concerned friend, I don't care, I need to know what's wrong and how I can fix it.

I push myself on the water today, paddling for over two hours. When I get home I still have an unfamiliar nervous energy coursing through me, so I head back out for a run in the twilight. Finally my body has had enough, and I fall asleep shortly after getting home and showering. It's a lot earlier than I normally go to bed, but trying to make sense of Mila and I is as emotionally exhausting as my strenuous workouts are physically exhausting. Some time later, I'm in the middle of a bizarre dream involving dancing parrots and a trumpet that talks, when the shrill sound of my phone ringing jolts me awake. I fumble for it on my nightstand. Mila's name flashes on the call display, and I immediately tap to answer.

"Mila? Are you okay?" I ask groggily, fighting back a yawn.

"Jackson? I need you, it's Milo. Something's wrong." She's crying, and the hysteria in her voice startles me to full alertness immediately. "He started limping earlier, and when I went to take him out to use the bathroom tonight, he yelped when he tried to walk. Now he's just lying on his side and he won't get up."

"I'm on my way."

I don't bother waiting for her response before ending the call and rushing out of bed and into a pair of sweats and a T-shirt. Thankfully, I've still got a bag of supplies and equipment in my car from a house call I did after clinic hours for an elderly couple who can't bring their cat to the clinic easily. It takes me less than five minutes from the time she called and I'm in my car speeding through the night to Mila's house. Milo's leg seemed like it was healing well, so hearing that he's in so much pain has me really worried.

I pull into her driveway, not caring that I'm parked crookedly. I do remember to close my car door gently, since I doubt her neighbours want to be awake at two am any more than I do. But right now Milo, and Mila, are more important than sleep.

I don't bother knocking, twisting the door handle in hopes that she's unlocked it. She has. Inside, the lights are low and I can hear her voice speaking softly from the kitchen. I walk swiftly down the hall to find her on the floor beside Milo's bed. She looks up at me with tears streaming down her face.

"Help him, Jackson." Her voice is broken, so I drop a kiss to her head before assessing Milo.

He's on his side, and for the first time since I met the dog, he doesn't get up to come and greet me. That alone tells me something is wrong. I check his breathing and his heart rate. Both seem to be normal, although slightly elevated. Which is to be expected if he's in pain.

"What did you guys do today?" I ask, partly to distract Mila from her worry, but more importantly to try and get a sense of what could have caused his pain and distress.

"I took him to work, we went for a walk on my lunch break, then after the bakery closed, we went down to the beach. He was limping a bit when we got home, but I didn't think it was anything serious. When we got home he laid down on his bed and he hasn't moved since then. He wouldn't even eat dinner. I thought I could wait and bring him in to the clinic tomorrow, but when he yelped earlier, I panicked. I'm sorry for waking you up."

I stop what I'm doing and turn to her. "Don't apologize. I'm glad you called me. Not just because I'm Milo's vet, but because I care about both of you."

She gives me a watery smile and I turn back to the dog lying before me. I continue to run my hands over his body, checking his front legs, both of which seem to be fine, and his torso. He gives my arm a small lick and the simple gesture of trust makes me smile. But that smile turns to a frown when I reach his back leg, the one that was injured, and I feel the inflammation in his joint.

"He's definitely strained his bad leg somehow." I go to mobilize his leg, and Milo whimpers. Mila drops her head down to his and starts to whisper to him. Whatever she's doing calms him, so I start to gently massage the area, pushing some of the swelling out of the area so I can get a better feel for the joint underneath. Slowly but surely, I work at it until I can move his leg with a bit more ease. I stand up and go to the freezer, looking for an ice pack. Finding one, I grab the dish towel from where it hangs on the oven door, wrap up the ice pack, and hold it on his leg.

"Can you hold this here for a minute?" I ask Mila. She places her hand where mine was on the ice pack, and I go to my bag for a tensor bandage. When that's loosely wrapped around the ice pack, keeping it securely in place, I rummage around for the pain killers I know I have with me. Standing back up, I slice some cheese I find in the fridge, remembering it as Milo's favourite treat, and then I try to tempt him to take the medicine.

"It's kind of funny how comfortable you are in my kitchen." Mila's offhand observation is said with a small smile, and I'm relieved to see she's a lot less upset than when I first arrived.

"Sorry, I should have asked before I just started grabbing stuff."

She touches my arm lightly, but I feel the warmth in my soul. "No, I like the fact that you just got what you needed. We're friends."

"Yeah. Friends." Not for the first time, that damn word leaves a strange feeling behind. "I'm going to go and check my car for a sling. We might need to help Milo stay off his leg for a few days to rest it."

Mila nods, her eyes downcast on Milo, and I head outside. In the cool, dark night, I take in a deep breath and blow it all out, feeling the adrenaline rush slowly fade. Thank God it wasn't something more serious. I want to get an x-ray of Milo's leg, just to be sure, but that can wait until tomorrow.

When I walk back into the kitchen, what I find makes me freeze mid-step. Mila's leaning against the cabinets just like she was when I left, but her eyes are closed, and it looks like she has fallen asleep. Milo is stretched out beside her, but he doesn't look as uncomfortable anymore. I unstrap the ice pack, not wanting to leave it on too long. Then I move his food and water bowl close by before stooping down low and lifting Mila into my arms.

"Jackson?" she says sleepily, and I kiss her head.

"Shh. Let me get you to bed. Milo will be fine now."

She makes an adorable soft noise of content and nestles into my arms. I walk the short distance to her bedroom and manage to lay her down on the mattress. I pull the blanket up and turn to leave when her voice stops me.

"Stay." When I look back, her eyes are open, and she's looking right at me. "Please. Just hold me."

I nod, afraid to say anything. I pull off my T-shirt but leave my sweats on, and slide in beside her on the bed. She turns over and curls up into my side, her head on my shoulder and her hand resting on my chest. I feel her take a deep breath in and out.

"Thank you for coming," she says quietly, her fingers drawing circles on my chest. "I was so scared."

My arm tightens around her. "I don't blame you. And I meant it when I said I'm glad you called. You and Milo are really important to me."

She lifts her head slightly to look at me, and her scrutiny almost makes me uncomfortable. I worry she can tell that what I just said is only a half truth. But she settles her head back down into the crook of my shoulder.

"Is this okay?"

Mila sounds nervous, and I frown slightly. "What, me staying?" She nods. "Yeah. It's fine."

"You're a really good friend, Jackson." The longing I can detect in her voice seems to mirror the hollowness of my own. It's becoming clear that neither one of us is really feeling the *just friends* part of our agreement.

Several moments pass and I wonder if she has fallen back asleep. My earlier exhaustion disappeared the second I heard her crying on the phone. Dealing with an emergency always causes a rush of adrenaline and I know it will be a while before I can sleep. Besides, the part of me that is a sucker for punishment is reveling in the feel of laying next to her, holding her once more. Even if it doesn't last past tonight.

But what if it could last longer...

That thought floats around my head for a while before finally, the comfort of Mila in my arms makes me drift off to sleep as well.

# CHAPTER SEVENTEEN

*Mila*

My alarm is accompanied by a deep groan that definitely does not come from me. Years of being an early riser has me conditioned to snap to full alertness at the first beep, but today there is a solid weight over my side, and a warm body pressed close enough behind me to make a certain situation very apparent. My back naturally arches into a stretch, rubbing against Jackson in a way that could easily lead to something if I didn't have a bakery to run. And if he actually wanted me that way.

"Fucking hell, it's early," he grumbles against my neck. I can tell the second he realizes his hand is cupping my breast, because his whole body freezes. "Sorry. I guess I got a little...close." A huff of warm air hits my bare shoulder. I twist in his arms to turn and face him, ignoring the fact that I instantly miss the feel of his hand on me.

"It's okay. You were comforting me."

His lips tip up into a smile that is pure sin. "Sure. I needed to cup your perfect breast to comfort you."

"You think my breasts are perfect?" I ask daringly.

Jackson doesn't answer right away. He tucks a piece of my hair behind my ear, his fingers trailing across my cheek. "I think *you* are perfect."

He leans in and kisses me lightly. I'm struck dumb. I have absolutely no idea how to respond. He's blurring the lines that he set between us, and I don't know what to do. Just as I start to psych myself up enough to ask him what he's thinking, he turns over and climbs out of bed.

"I'm going to check on Milo," he says over his shoulder as he walks out of the room.

I scramble to get up as well, instantly feeling guilty that my poor dog wasn't my first thought. I follow him into the kitchen, and Milo gets up from his bed slowly to walk over to us. He's putting weight on all four legs, but still limping. I bend down and give him some love while Jackson lifts a fabric sling off the table, then hooks it under Milo's belly.

"This will help him avoid putting too much weight on that leg for a while," he explains as he slowly leads Milo to the back door. I trail behind, watching the man I'm falling for care for my silly dog with such tenderness it warms my heart. My coffee maker beeps, making me turn back inside. I set out two mugs and head back into my room to quickly get dressed. When I come back into the kitchen, Milo is eating some kibble and Jackson is pouring milk into two mugs of coffee. He's still only wearing low slung navy blue sweatpants, and I admire the muscular lines of his back openly while he isn't looking. Jackson

Holt is one beautiful man. The second he turns around I move my gaze elsewhere. I'm confused, and unsure of where we stand. But one thing is for certain, I'm incredibly grateful to the man in front of me.

"Thanks for staying last night, I was kind of a mess," I say honestly, taking a sip of the coffee he hands me. My eyes follow him as he walks even closer to me. He stops when he's directly in front of me, and good lord, he's close. Why does he smell so good first thing in the morning? That doesn't seem fair. My hand itches to reach out and touch his bare skin, to fold myself back into his arms and let him hold me.

But I don't. Instead I hold my coffee between us like it's some kind of shield. "I've got to get to the bakery and start prepping everything."

He takes a casual sip of his coffee, acting oblivious to the sexual tension that I feel thrumming through me. He must feel it. There's no way I imagined the hard length of his cock pressed against me this morning.

"What are you baking?" he asks. Maybe the sparks I feel jumping between us are all in my head. I'm starting to feel completely crazy.

"The usual. Triple berry scones, lemon poppyseed muffins," I reply. "Maybe some bran muffins to say thank you again to a certain vet."

His eyes flare slightly. "You don't have to keep thanking me. But I certainly won't turn away bran muffins."

We both stand there, sipping coffee and staring at each other. I can't figure out if he's five seconds away from stripping my clothes off, or five seconds away from walking out the door. I'm so confused by this man.

"Do you want to come with me?" I blurt out the question quickly, without thinking if I want him to say yes or no.

But when his smile covers his face, I'm filled with a similar happiness. "I would love to. Are you going to teach me the secret muffin recipe?"

I pretend to look offended. "Never. That goes with me to the grave."

He chuckles, takes my empty mug and sets it in the sink behind him. "Fine. I'll settle for the not-so-secret recipe."

Being alone with Jackson in my kitchen this early in the morning feels oddly intimate. I know we've had sex, and last night we slept together, but his presence here during my early morning rituals is different somehow. These hours are usually my form of meditation. My way to process the previous day, prepare for the present day, and dream of the future.

"Can you hand me the raisins, please?"

Jackson reaches over and grabs the container I'm pointing to, and places it on the counter in front of me.

"Did you know I've never had raisins in a bran muffin before yours?"

I smile fondly, keeping my attention on the bowl of muffin batter in front of me. "It was a tip given to me by my Aunt Marilyn. She said raisins would add the sweetness that bran muffins were always missing."

"She was a smart woman." Jackson picks a raisin out of the container and pops it in his mouth.

"She *is*. She taught my mom how to bake, and mom taught me. I remember she would come to town for a weekend and the three of us would do nothing but make a mess in the kitchen, experimenting with flavour combos and creating dozens of muffins and scones." Memories of those days come flooding back, and as always happens when I think of my parents, I'm filled with happiness for the time I had with them, and grief over losing out on so much. They died way too soon.

"How is it that you can make the best bread I've ever tasted, scones and muffins that would make a pastry chef weep, but you claim you can't make cookies?"

I lift my hands in the universal sign for "who knows". "It's a mystery. Every time I try to follow a cookie recipe, they come out as hard as hockey pucks. It's safer for everyone if I just leave the cookie baking to Kelly."

Jackson nods and takes another raisin, and I swat his hand away. "Stay out of the ingredients, mister."

He just chuckles and when my hands go back to the bowl in front of me, the sneak takes another.

Over the next hour or so, Jackson helps me prepare all of the muffin batter, get the bread loaves in the oven, and somehow, he convinces me to make cinnamon buns as well. Having him at the bakery with me is nice. He takes care of Milo when the dog needs to go out, and the time flies by with our easy conversation. But at the same time, I struggle to make sense of what's happening. Something has clearly changed for him; even before when we added sex to our agreement he was not this openly flirtatious and affectionate. The little touches at the small of my back when he walks past me, fleeting kisses to my head, and the way he looks at me every now and then — all leave me feeling warm and flustered. I want to ask him what he's thinking, but I also don't want to ruin it. Because the needy, aroused part of me is just basking in the extra attention like his cat Harley basks in the sunshine.

When Kelly arrives, she doesn't even bat an eye at Jackson's presence, as if he's been there many times before. We discuss the cookie flavours for the day, I write up the menu board, and she gets to work. As the morning goes on and the rest of my staff arrive, I know Jackson will have to leave. And when the time comes, he stands up from the stool he occupied for most of the morning and wraps his arms around me.

"This was fun," he says quietly.

I nod against his chest, inhaling his comforting, sexy, all-masculine smell deeply.

When we separate, he picks up the box I filled with muffins and scones for the clinic staff and heads to the back door. He pets Milo, gives me one last smile and leaves.

"That man is crazy for you."

Kelly's voice startles me out of the trance I fell into watching Jackson leave.

"What? Oh. Yeah, well, you know." I stammer out a reply. "He's a great guy," I say lamely.

"Mmhmm." She gives me a knowing look. "Pretty easy on the eyes, too."

I blush. "Very easy."

We both giggle and get back to work, but the warm feeling inside of me doesn't fade for a long time.

Later on, I'm out front, wandering through the front of the bakery, chatting with a few customers when Riley and Dean come through the door. Riley is beaming, and Dean looks incredibly happy.

"Hey you two, what's going on?"

Riley beckons me closer, so I crouch down to her level. Her eyes are glistening with what I assume are happy tears. "We met with a high-risk OB-GYN yesterday who specializes in spinal cord injury patients. He agreed we could try to have a baby."

I pull her in for a hug. Riley's dreamt of having a baby for years, but her health was precarious for a while. Hearing that she's stable enough to try and conceive feels like a miracle. A well-deserved miracle.

"That's fantastic news. Muffins are on the house today, guys." I stand up and hug Dean before going to the case and taking out two apple nut muffins and putting them on a plate for my friends. I drop off the goodies and head back to the kitchen to keep working on the cinnamon buns Jackson convinced me to make. I think I'll drop one off at the clinic for him later. As I'm putting them in the oven, my brother sticks his head in the kitchen.

"Hey Mills, can you come next door and look at something?"

"Yup." I load the tray of buns into the oven, set the timer, and follow Ethan through the bakery and into the future café. A plastic barrier covers the opening between the two spaces, and Ethan has done a great job keeping the noisy jobs to a minimum during the hours the bakery is open. It's been a couple of days since I was in here, and the changes are incredible. The floors have been refinished, and the walls are painted the same soft butter yellow as the bakery side. The furniture I ordered is stacked against one wall, and the deli counter is installed. I run my hands over everything as I wander around in awe.

"Ethan. This is amazing."

He comes to stand beside me and drapes his arm over my shoulders. "You did it, Mills."

I nod, my head resting against his shoulder. "We did it. Seriously, Ethan, I could never have done this without you." His arm squeezes me gently.

"Mom would be so thrilled with this place."

Tears spring to my eyes. "I wish she was here."

"She is. They both are."

We stand there quietly for a moment, united in our grief in a way no one else can possibly understand. My brother has been my rock for years. Our loss brought us closer than most other siblings will ever be, and for a long time he has been everything to me. Friend, confidant, protector. But when his phone vibrates and he pulls it out, and I see Summer's name on the screen, his arm falls away from me and I realize I'm not everything to him anymore.

He's found the love of his life, and rightly so, she is his priority now.

So, whose priority am I?

# Chapter Eighteen

*Jackson*

There is no point in denying it any longer. My feelings for Mila are real, and I want her in my life. I want to spend the night with her, wake up with her...hell, I even want to spend more mornings at the bakery with her even if I am feeling absolutely exhausted by the early afternoon.

I've got a break between patients, so I close the door to the office, and lay my head down on the desk. Just a few minutes and I'll be fine.

Mila's voice saying my name softly penetrates through the fog of sleep and in my half-awake state, my arm lifts up on its own accord to wrap around her body. I tug her in close, hearing her low laugh.

"I don't know how you survive those early mornings day after day," I mumble, blinking up at her. She strokes my hair, and this quiet moment feels so natural, even though there's no one around.

"Well, I'm not normally up until midnight with my dog."

Reluctantly I move my hand from her waist and stand up to stretch. Out of the corner of my eye I watch Mila, and her gaze doesn't leave me. That's when I see what she's set down on the desk.

"Is that for me?" I unwrap the plate holding one of her massive cinnamon buns and my mouth starts to water. "You're ruining me. What bran muffin can compete with this?"

"Maybe the two you ate this morning?" she teases right back. I rub my stomach and grin at her.

"I don't know what you're talking about." She shakes her head as I take a large bite of the cinnamon bun, then tear off a piece and hold it out to her. "You need to have some."

Mila's eyes flare as she opens her mouth. I put the piece of bun inside, and she lets out a soft moan that has my dick stirring in my pants.

"That's really good." She reaches across me to tear off another piece and pops it in her mouth with a smile.

"You should know, you made it." My voice is husky. I had no idea cinnamon buns could be so damn sexy.

Things are shifting between us. I know I need to man up and talk to her about the fact that I want to make things official between us, but that means opening myself up for rejection. Before I found out that Stefani cheated on me, I would have probably laughed at myself for even considering the idea of Mila cheating. Every sign is pointing to her being attracted to me, and things are definitely getting a lot more serious between us. But if I could be so wrong about my ex, could I be wrong about Mila?

My phone rings, and when I glance down, I see it's my mom. "I have to get this, but can you wait for me?" Mila nods and I answer the phone.

"Hey, Mom. I'm just at work, is everything okay?" I don't break eye contact with Mila, watching as she fidgets with her bag.

"Hi sweetie. I won't keep you long, just wanted to see if you could possibly get the day after tomorrow off to show your parents around? I know it's short notice, but we wanted to surprise you and come to the island tomorrow. Your dad convinced me to give you some warning so you could get some time off work."

The excitement in her voice makes me smile and ignore the fact that this is really not great timing. "That sounds awesome, Mom. I can't wait to show you around."

My mother chatters in my ear for another few minutes before I get her off the phone with promises to talk with Phil about switching shifts. When I hang up the phone, Mila looks ready to bolt. But I'm not about to let that happen.

"Sounds like you're going to be busy this weekend," she says, her eyes darting everywhere.

"So are you."

Her head whips around to look at me so quickly I'm surprised she doesn't get whiplash. "Why me? We don't have to pretend with your parents."

"No. I don't want to lie to them. But I do want them to meet the woman who is responsible for my happiness here." My palms sweat just saying that, but her answering smile washes over me, warm like the sun.

"I'd like that."

"Great. Dinner at my house tomorrow? Bring Milo, my dad loves dogs." When she nods, I mentally pump my fist in the air. Dinner at my house is nothing new, but introducing her to my parents is. I wish I could introduce her as my girlfriend, not just my friend, but all in good time.

"I should go. I need to walk Milo." But she makes no move to leave.

"How is he doing?" I ask, leaning against the desk. I know I probably have patients waiting, but I'm in no rush to have her go.

"His limp was way better when I took him out at lunch time." She smiles up at me, and I lie to myself and say the tenderness there is for me, not for her dog. "You'll have to teach me the massage you did. It really seemed to help."

The mental picture I have when I put the words *Mila* and *massage* together is not one I want to share right now. There's a knock at the door, and Rosie pokes her head in.

"Sorry to interrupt, Doctor Holt, but your next patient is waiting in exam room two."

I stand up from the desk. "Thanks Rosie, I'll be right there."

Mila heads to the door but I catch her quickly, taking her hand in mine. "Let me walk you out."

Rosie places her hand on her heart and tips her head at us. "Oh goodness, you two are so sweet together."

I look at Mila and as I expected, she's blushing. I squeeze her hand and refrain from saying anything else. Out front it's a different story. The waiting room is full, and when all eyes turn to us, I see her turn even more pink. Little does she know how fucking sexy I think that is.

I hold the door open for her and as she walks past, I take her chin in my hand and tip her face up to mine. I place a lingering but entirely workplace appropriate kiss on her lips, loving the little gasp she makes when our lips connect.

"See you tomorrow."

Dinner tonight is going to be special, for more than one reason, I hope. When I approached Phil about trading our shifts for tomorrow, he agreed easily. Then he handed me an envelope, and with a firm handshake told me to take the time to read it over and give him an answer when I'm next in the office. Without him saying it, I know exactly what's inside. An offer to purchase half of the clinic and officially become his partner. I didn't expect to receive the offer so soon; it's only been a few months. But I know deep in my soul that this is the right place for me to be, and I don't mean just because of my career.

I picked my parents up at the ferry terminal and made the drive to Dogwood Cove, listening to my mom catch me up on all the things that have happened back home — no, not back home. Where they live. Dogwood Cove is home for me now.

When it's my turn to talk, my mother doesn't waste any time reading between the lines. "Every single story you've told us has this Mila woman in it. Is there something we need to know?" She angles her body to face me from the passenger seat of my car, and my dad groans from the back seat.

"For God's sake, Anne, give the boy a break. You haven't seen him in months and you're already grilling him."

Mom reaches back to swat at him while I hide my grin.

"I'm not grilling him, I just want to know more about the woman who has put a smile back on my son's face," she replies indignantly before looking at me again. "Do we get to meet her?"

"As a matter of fact, you do. She's coming over for dinner tonight," I reply. Mom claps her hands in delight and proceeds to badger me for all the details about Mila.

Yep, she's gonna love her.

An hour later, my parents have fallen in love with Dogwood Cove. When Mom saw the gazebo at the center of town, she freaked out. Apparently it looks just like the gazebo in some show about a mother and daughter that I would have sworn she's too old to enjoy. Not that I say that to her, of course.

We're at my house, and I'm pouring a glass of wine for my mom when there's a knock on my door.

"I'll get it!" My mother says in a voice that's a little too high pitched.

"Mom. Chill, please?" I call after her, knowing it won't do any good.

I hear her greet Mila, and exclaim over whatever tray of deliciousness Mila brought with her. They walk into the kitchen, and my mom's arm is threaded through Mila's and they're both laughing. Milo comes trotting in after them and heads straight for my dad, as if he knows who the other dog lover is.

That was easy.

Mila sets down the plate she's carrying and walks over to me. I put my arm around her shoulders and kiss the side of her head. "Hey, thanks for coming. Wine?" I ask casually, ignoring the fact that my mom is watching the two of us, and I'm pretty sure her eyes are shining.

"So, Mila, Jackson says you're responsible for him feeling so...*welcome* in town." The innuendo couldn't be any stronger, and Mom picks up her wine glass and sips it innocently. I narrow my eyes at her.

"Oh, umm, yeah. Well, he's a great guy." Mila sputters, grabbing the glass I hand her and taking a large swallow. I place my hand on the small of her back and decide to take pity on her. After all, she doesn't know that I've decided I want to make things real between us. I guess I can understand why my mother's excitement is confusing.

"Mom, we're just friends. I told you." I chide gently.

Mom just smiles at us over her wine glass. "Mmhmm. Just friends. Right. I heard you," she says mildly.

I roll my eyes and head out to the grill to pull dinner off. We dish up chicken, salad, and fresh corn on the cob and sit down to eat.

Conversation turns to Mila's expansion, and when my dad hears that she's been experimenting with a soft pretzel recipe, his ears perk right up.

"I'll make some tomorrow after I finish the baking for the day," Mila says with a smile.

"You're a keeper, Mila," my dad says, patting her shoulder and giving me a raised eyebrow.

I see Mila look at the clock; it's well after eight pm.

"Well, I should be going so you guys can settle in." She stands up and goes to gather her things. My mom shoots daggers at me before jumping up and grabbing Mila's arm. I don't know what I did to piss off Mom, but I think Mila leaving has something to do with it.

"Oh, honey, don't leave on our account. We got a last-minute cancellation at that new place on the beach," my mom says. "You two stay and enjoy each other. Have some more wine."

"Oh my God, Mom." I groan at her innuendo.

Mila smiles, but her eyes dart up to me and they hold some uncertainty that I'm even more determined to erase after seeing how easily she gets along with my parents. "You'll love it there, Anne. My best friend runs the place."

"How lovely," Mom beams, and pulls Mila in for a hug. "It's just so nice to meet you. I'm making Jackson bring us to the bakery for breakfast tomorrow. We'll see you then."

She turns to me and wraps her arms around my middle. "Bye, sweetie. See you tomorrow." Then she pulls my head down to her level to kiss my cheek, and she whispers quietly, "Just friends, huh? Fix that, Jackson Holt."

My parents leave, and then it's just Mila and I. My mother's parting words linger with me. *Fix it, Jackson.*

"Sorry about their enthusiasm for us. They don't claim to be subtle," I joke.

"Your parents are wonderful."

Something passes between us, and I know what I need to do. I walk over to my bag from work and pull out the envelope Phil gave me. Waving it at Mila, I say, "I'm pretty sure this is some good news. Stay for another glass and celebrate?"

She looks at the clock and I can see the indecision.

"Please, Mila." I'm not above begging. I need her to stay.

"Okay. But only a small one," she capitulates. I grin, pour some wine and take her hand to lead her back to the deck. We sit down on the chairs after I pull mine to be right next to hers, and I finally open the letter.

"It is my honour to present you with an offer to purchase half ownership of the Dogwood Cove Veterinary Clinic," I read, a grin stretching across my face. I look at Mila, and she's smiling, but it's tinged with something else. "We did it. I got the partnership."

"That's great, Jackson, I'm so happy." She sips her wine and I put the letter down before taking the glass from her hands and setting it on the table.

"Are you?"

She laughs, but won't meet my eyes. "Of course. You got your partnership, my café is almost ready to open — we both got what we wanted, so now we can end the charade and stop lying to everyone."

I take a minute to figure out exactly what to say. I need to make sure she hears me perfectly. Slowly I lift my hands, taking in the way she follows my movement with a wary look in her eyes. I cup her cheeks, my thumbs stroking her soft skin gently. When she finally meets my gaze, I feel my lips turn up.

"You're right. We can stop lying to everyone else. But I want you to know, I've stopped lying to myself as well. I want you, Mila. I don't want to end our relationship, but I do want to end the charade and make it real between us."

# Chapter Nineteen

*Mila*

Did he really just say that? I stare at Jackson, at those beautiful blue eyes that have the ability to heat me up. His hands are holding mine, and the connection is infusing me with such certainty, such joy, I don't exactly know what to do. My heart feels like the Grinch on Christmas day, growing three sizes in an instant. This man, who wants the same things as I do, who makes me feel *more* than I ever have, wants me.

"Are you...Are you sure? You really want to..." I can't formulate a complete sentence to save my life, and it turns out I don't have to, because Jackson leans in and kisses me. But this isn't the chaste, simple kisses we've been sharing since we ended the sexual part of whatever we had going on.

No, this is a kiss that promises so much more. His tongue is tracing the seam of my mouth and I open for him. His answering groan of pleasure sends tingles down my spine and I let go of his hands so I can thread mine in his hair. He lifts me out of my seat and guides me to straddle his lap, our mouths barely losing contact. My head slants to the side, pressing deeper into him. He's plundering my mouth, and I don't want this kiss to ever end. Slowly I become aware of other things. Like the fact that I can feel his cock through his shorts and the friction between my thighs as I rub shamelessly back and forth is making me breathless. Desperate need fills me. I need to feel him, to have him. For real.

"Stay," he murmurs. "Stay with me tonight."

I don't answer, at least not with words. I lean back and peel off my shirt, exposing the blue lace bra I have on underneath.

"Mila," Jackson growls, his hands coming up to cup my breasts. "Do your panties match?" The wicked gleam in his eyes tells me he has every intention of finding out and his deliciously gruff tone makes me shiver.

"You'll see," is my throaty reply.

His lips go to my collarbone, gently sucking and kissing his way up the column of my neck. I twist slightly, needing his mouth on mine like I need air to breathe.

"You're mine. You get that, right?"

I pull back, to see banked heat in Jackson's eyes. "Yes," I whisper.

One word is all it takes to unleash him. It's as if a light switch was hit the second we admitted things were real between us. Gone is the sexy but reserved Jackson. He was an incredible lover, attentive and giving, but the man roaming his hands and lips all over my body now is like an uncaged beast. He stands up with me wrapped around him, and stalks inside.

"Wait, the dog," I protest.

He freezes, pivots back to the door, and barks out a command. "Milo. Come." My dog trots inside, and he must sense now is not the time to disturb us because he goes straight to the couch, climbs onto it and curls up in a ball. Jackson carries me to his bedroom and lays me down on his bed, his hands running down my sides. Then with a voice that drips with lust, he says, "Your turn. Mila, Come." That's all the warning I get before he bends down and kisses a line down my stomach, reaching my shorts and making swift work of removing them. He pauses for a second, staring at my panties before looking up at me with a hot grin. "Matching. I knew it." He peels them down slowly, his lips trailing his hands with some kisses pressed over my heated skin. I let my head fall back and close my eyes, ready for the pleasure I know he's about to give me when that commanding tone is back.

"Open your eyes."

I look down to see his face between my legs, and there's more than just simple lust written on his face.

"I want to you to watch me. Watch me devour you, claim you, love you."

I know it's just a choice of words. He doesn't really mean he loves me. But still, *this is real now.* This isn't just two friends having casual sex. This is two people who share a real connection, with real feelings, making real love. The intensity of that realization hits me at the same time as his tongue hits my clit and together, the two make me cry out his name.

His hands grip my hips tighter, holding me in place as I start to move under his touch. He's doing wicked things with his tongue, drawing circles around my clit, sucking it into his mouth until I'm panting.

"That. Whatever you're doing. Keep doing it."

His low chuckle vibrates against my sensitized skin, making me moan. When I feel a finger probing at my entrance, my hips arch up, inviting him in. He adds a second, stretching me, then he curls his fingers, hitting the perfect spot right away, like magic. He strokes back and forth, teasing me. I barely recognize the sounds coming out of my mouth, and his other arm comes up to lay across my stomach to stop my writhing and hold me in place. My breaths are coming quicker and quicker, my heart is racing, and my hands are holding his head tightly when all at once I detonate. My orgasm washes over me with all the subtlety of a tidal wave.

"Jackson. Jackson. Jackson. Jackson." I'm chanting his name over and over as my body shudders through a release that holds all of the pent-up emotion, and lust, and need I've had building over the last few weeks. When it subsides, I slowly come back to earth and back to the reality of Jackson beside me, his hand drawing patterns on my bare stomach. He's still wearing clothes, which simply won't do. I muster up the energy to roll over and undo the button and zipper on his shorts.

"Mila, I need you." His voice is hoarse, thick with emotion. But I shake my head and shift my body down to his side. I let my fingers dance over the ridges of his abs, grinning when I feel him tense up as I hit a ticklish spot. His body feels like my own personal playground and I'm finally free to play. As his rigid cock is freed from his clothes, my tongue darts out to lick my lips. Keeping my eyes on Jackson's face, I position myself between his legs. I grip his thigh in one hand, feeling the coarse hairs and the bunched muscles. The other hand wraps around his thick length. My fingers just barely meet, and the memory of all of him inside me makes me shiver. I move in a few light strokes up and down, feeling the silky skin of his tip, and the ridges of his shaft.

"Fuck. Babe." He's clutching the sheets beside him, and I frown. I don't want him to hold back. I bow my head and take him into my mouth as deep as I can. His hands come the back of my head, and I smile. That's better. He starts to guide my movements, with the perfect amount of respectful control. I quickly remember what drives him wild, using my tongue to swirl around the tip in between long licks and sucks. I move one hand from his thigh round to cup his balls, playing with them gently, earning a long, low growl of pleasure.

"Come here."

Suddenly two hands are lifting me up. I settle on Jackson's hips, his cock nestled between the folds of my sex, his fingers digging into me. The fire in his eyes tells me everything. I bend down and kiss him, slowly tangling my tongue with his, pouring all of my emotion into this one kiss. He meets me stroke for stroke, our breath mingling together. Then he flips me onto my back, pushes my legs apart and thrusts into me in one movement.

"Oh God, yes," I breathe, arching up into him. He captures one of my nipples in his mouth as his hips start to move.

"Shit. Wait." Jackson freezes above me, breathing heavily. "We need a condom."

He slides out of me, and leans over to grab one from the drawer of his bedside table. His fingers are fumbling, probably from having to stop so suddenly. It's cute, but I need him to hurry the fuck up. My fingers drift down to play with my clit. The second he realizes what I'm doing, Jackson swats away my hand.

"No. Mine."

I cock my head and smirk at him. "Okay, caveman. Then hurry up."

He lunges back over me, grabs one of my legs, lifting it up over his shoulder before he slides slowly into my throbbing heat. "I don't want to hurry. I want this to last forever."

The raw words hit me square in the chest, making my heart squeeze. Jackson drops his head down to meet mine, as he moves at an agonizing pace, grinding against me with every thrust. Warm waves of pleasure hit me one after the other, making my pleasure coil tighter than a spring. He nuzzles into my neck, kissing my heated skin. I can hear he's muttering something, but I can't make it out over the buzzing in my ears from my impending orgasm. I'm clutching at him, digging my nails into his skin, when his hands take mine and lift them over my head, trapping them in place. "Oh God, yes, Jackson, I'm so close. So...close." His hips pick up the pace, moving in and out of me, stroking every inch of me. The change in position is apparently all that my body needs. I clench around him, and his answering groan sends me impossibly higher until we're crying out each others names as our orgasms take over.

The alarm on my phone has been going off for several seconds before I manage to muster the energy to turn it off. Parts of my body are deliciously sore from the three, or was it four, orgasms Jackson gave me last night. I'm exhausted, but happy. So, so, so happy.

I turn over in his arms, and his grip around me tightens.

"Mmm. We have to get up, don't we," he mumbles into my hair.

I smile, bringing my hand up to cup his cheek. "I do. You don't. Come in for a muffin later."

He groans and stretches his body, bringing every naked inch into even closer contact with me. "No, you get up, I get up. That's how this works, babe."

For some reason the fact that he's willing to wake up so early with me, just because, means a lot. I've never had anyone in my life who wanted to do that.

But I know I'm more of a morning person than he is, simply because I'm used to it. So I push back the covers and sit up. But his arm wraps around my middle and tugs me back down.

"Five more minutes?" His tone is so adorably pleading, I comply with a giggle, laying back down and snuggling into his arms.

"Only five."

We lay there in the early morning stillness. His arms are banded around me, holding me close, and everything feels so perfectly right. Suddenly a furry weight jumps onto the bed, and Harley starts to knead the covers on Jackson's chest.

"Dammit, cat, it's too early," he groans.

"Sorry," I giggle. "I guess he heard my alarm."

Jackson pushes the cat away and sits up. "That's fine. We'll all get used to the new schedule."

The way he says it makes me think he plans on being with me overnight a lot, and the thought makes me smile. Seeing his naked ass when he stands up and goes toward the bathroom doesn't hurt, either. He must sense me staring, because he turns in the doorway and braces his hands on the top of the frame, unashamedly displaying his delicious body.

"Like what you see, babe?"

I nod slowly, and he prowls back over to me. When he's standing in front of me, his hands go under my arms and he lifts me up, straight into his arms.

"If you're gonna stare at me like that, at least do it in the shower so we can multitask."

I shriek and hang on tightly as he walks us into the bathroom, not setting me down until I'm in the shower with every inch of his naked body in front of me. He blocks the spray of water until the temperature is perfect, then he turns me so the water cascades over my body.

"You look like you're going to devour me," I say, taking in his hooded eyes that prowl over my body.

"I want to."

His words send a shiver of anticipation down my spine. But then he picks up the shampoo, squirts some into his hands, and starts washing my hair.

"What happened to devouring me?" I place my hands on my hips in a mock pout, even as I feel my shoulders relax under the feel of his hands massaging my hair.

His lips kiss my neck, dragging their way up to my ear. "If I took the time that I need to devour you, no one would get any muffins today." I'm about to protest that I don't give a shit about muffins right now, when he continues. "I promise I'll make it up to you tonight."

He tips my head back under the water to rinse my hair, and I arch my back. My eyes are closed, so I don't realize what he's doing until his lips close around my nipple, making me gasp.

"I thought you said we didn't have time."

"I just need a taste," he mutters against my skin. My hands go to the back of his head, trapping him in place. God, I could come just from his mouth on my breast.

"Jackson." His name comes out as a needy plea, and he takes pity on me.

"Oh!" I cry out as his fingers plunge inside of me. He moves quickly, thumbing my clit, sucking on my breast, and playing me up and over the edge within minutes. I sag into his arms, breathing heavily, my skin feeling every drop of water, it's so sensitive right now.

"I thought you said we didn't have time?" I manage to say eventually, opening my eyes to see him smirking.

"I was too hungry to wait."

# Chapter Twenty

*Jackson*

To the rest of the world, nothing has changed between Mila and I. But to us, everything has. I feel it and I know she does, too. Her smile is bigger, and her arms hold me tighter when she hugs me in public. And I can kiss her, not that I couldn't before, but now I can linger. I can taste and savour her, kissing her long and deep until she pulls back with that beautiful pink flush covering her cheeks.

And I'm happy. Happier than I can ever remember. Thanks, in no small part, to the incredible sex we have every night. I can honestly say I never knew I could feel this satisfied.

When her alarm goes off each morning, I walk with her to the bakery, then head out for a workout. Most days it's still warm enough to get out on the water for a paddle, but sometimes I go for a run. I'm starting to understand why Mila says she likes her early mornings. It is a peaceful feeling, like we are the only two people awake, and the world is ours.

We've been official for a few weeks, but it feels like so much longer, thanks to all the time we spent pretending. The conversation about whether or not we should come clean to our friends hasn't come up, and I'm grateful. I really just want to pretend that whole fake relationship shit never happened, and convince ourselves that we've always been this way. Deliriously happy and completely insatiable for each other.

"Honey, I'm home!" Mila walks into my kitchen where I'm popping the tops off of two bottles of craft beer. I hand one to her, leaning down for a kiss.

"You're ridiculous, you know that?" I mutter against her smile. Milo nudges my knee, and I pat his head. Truthfully, I kind of love how comfortable the two of them are here. Almost as much as I love how comfortable I am at her place. Sure, it's a bit crazy having clothing at two places, and half the time we forget something we really need that's at the other house, but it works. Neither one of us wants to rush things, so even if we are together all the time, we keep our own homes.

Later, over dinner, I slide an envelope across the table to her. She looks up from her bowl of seafood pasta with a curious smile teasing her lips.

"The last time you had an envelope to share with me it was your offer letter from Morton. What is it this time?"

I shrug. "Open it and find out." I have to fight back my own grin of excitement as she pulls out the reservation confirmation for a two-night stay at a luxury hotel on the mainland. It's situated right in the heart of BC's wine country, and I made sure to also book us a private wine tour.

"Jackson, what in the world?" Her eyes are shining when she meets my gaze.

"I've already worked it out with Kelly. She'll cover for you on Monday, and you're going to close a little early on Saturday so we can catch the ferry. Ethan and Summer will pet sit, all we have to do is sit back and relax for a couple of days."

She leans over and kisses me. "I'm beyond excited, but why?"

"Because I got partner at the clinic, because you're so close to opening the café, because you haven't taken any time off all summer, and because you deserve to be spoiled by the guy who's crazy about you."

Mila drops her fork down, pushes her chair back, and comes around the table to sit sideways in my lap. Her hands wrap around my neck and I see a tear slowly fall from her eyes. My thumb reaches up to gently caress it away.

"How did I get so lucky?"

Our lips touch. "You wooed me with muffins. I was powerless against your cinnamon buns. And your dog loves me." She starts to giggle, then full-on laugh, tossing her head back. When her laughter subsides, she looks at me, and the emotions I see beaming out of her take my breath away. She leans back down and feathers my face with light kisses before landing back on my lips.

"I still don't think I deserve you, but thank you," she whispers.

I push my chair back and lift her into my arms.

"Wait, where are we going? What about dinner?" Mila swats at my arm half-heartedly.

"We can come back to it. Right now, I apparently need to *prove* to you that you deserve everything and more."

Which I am more than happy to do, over and over until we fall asleep, dinner forgotten.

"Oh my God, it's so fancy," Mila says under her breath as we walk into the lobby of the hotel. I have to admit to some regret when she told me the story of Cole Devereaux, CEO of Devereaux Hotels International, trying to buy Oceanside Resort from Summer, and all the drama it caused with her and Ethan. But here we are, standing inside one of his luxury hotels, about to enjoy everything it has to offer.

"Are you sure Summer and Ethan are okay with us being here?" I ask, gripping the handle on my suitcase, ready to turn around and book us in a local motel if I have to.

"Yes, Jackson. Stop worrying. This is amazing — look at the fountain!" She points excitedly over to a water feature that I must admit is pretty over the top. The whole place is, but that's what I wanted for this weekend. She doesn't know about the spa package I set up for her, or the wine tour...yet. My plan is to keep the surprises coming until her head spins. Or until I get up the courage to tell her I'm falling in love with her.

That's the other reason for this trip. I want to say those words to her, and I want it to be special. Something we'll never forget.

Mila's excitement over everything is exactly what I hoped for. Our room is stunning, and the champagne I ordered is waiting in a bucket of ice. She flops facedown on the bed with a dreamy smile, and I sit down beside her, my hand coming to caress her leg.

"I might never want to leave."

"But then who would make my geriatric muffins?" I tease, stretching out on the bed beside her.

She reaches over and pokes me. "You haven't eaten a bran muffin in weeks."

"Only because my girlfriend hasn't bothered to save me one," I retort.

Mila lifts her head and props it on her hand. She pulls her lip in between her teeth and I reach up with my thumb to free it.

"I like that. You calling me your girlfriend."

The soft smile she gives me almost makes me blurt out the words *I love you* right then and there. But I don't. Not yet.

"Come on. Let's go into town and walk around before dinner." I stand up and hold my hand out to help her up. Of course, she doesn't need help, but it's the perfect set up to tug her into my arms and hold her. Which has become my favourite thing in the world, next to kissing her and making love to her.

"Only if my *boyfriend* pours a glass of champagne while I take a quick shower." Mila goes up on her toes and kisses my chin before spinning away and going into the bathroom. I hear the shower turn on and make quick work of popping open the champagne and pouring two glasses.

"I might need some help washing my back." Mila's voice makes me turn and I see her head peeking out the bathroom door, steam billowing around her hair, which is piled on top of her head. I walk over, glasses of champagne in hand. She pushes the door wide open, revealing her very naked body.

"Fuck, babe." The sight of her, as always, almost brings me to my knees. "Take these." I pass her the glasses, then strip off my clothes. By the time I get there, Mila's in the shower, which conveniently has a large bench at one end of the massive stall. Her head is tipped down as the water rains down on her shoulders. But when I open the door, she looks up at me with her intoxicating brown eyes. I lift my glass of champagne and take a sip, letting the cool, effervescent liquid slide down my throat. Her gaze drops as I swallow.

"How do you make everything so sexy?" she asks in a husky whisper. I step closer, bringing her body flush with mine. Leaning down, I nuzzle her neck before replying.

"I could ask you the same thing. One look from you and I'm undone."

"Jackson," she sighs as I pepper her skin with open-mouthed kisses, sucking lightly. My hand drifts down between her legs, sliding through her slick folds. "Yes..." Her hips arch into my hand, and I dip a finger inside. "More. Jackson, I need more."

I kiss her, hard, then spin her around to face the bench. "Bend down, babe." She complies immediately, and the position puts her luscious ass into the perfect position. Looking at me over her shoulder, Mila gives me a look of total trust and adoration that cracks my heart open even wider.

"I'm clean and I have an IUD. I want you bare." Her silky voice and those words almost make me lose control right then and there. But somehow I hold back.

"Are you sure? I'm clean, too. I got everything checked when I found out about Stef." As much as I hate to bring up my ex in this moment, she needs to know that I would never put her at risk.

In answer, Mila thrusts her hips back and widens her stance. "I'm sure, Jackson."

I place my hands on the globes of her ass, caressing the heated, wet skin. Bending down, my lips touch her spine, and she arches into my touch with a low moan.

"Please."

Taking my cock in hand, I line up with her entrance. My fingers already felt how wet she is, how ready for me she is, so when I push inside, she opens for me easily. I work my way in and out with shallow thrusts, paying attention to how her breathing speeds up. She reaches back with one hand, grabs mine and wraps it around to cup her breast. I'm bent over her back, and the angle is bringing me deeper and deeper.

"Oh God, yes, fuck. Right there," she pants, her hips moving to meet mine with every thrust.

"Goddamnit Mila. You feel so perfect," I growl. I squeeze her breast, pinching her nipple gently. "Fuck, I'm close, babe."

"So am I. So close."

The base of my spine starts to tingle as my balls tighten and I feel my control slipping. My movements get hurried, and soon I'm shouting out her name as her cries echo around us. My hands come up to the wall above her head to hold myself up. I can see her arms shaking so I summon the strength to gather her up into my arms, turn us around and sit down with her in my lap. She snuggles in, her hand coming up to drape around my neck.

"Mmm. We need a shower bench at home." Her voice drips with satisfaction and I chuckle.

"Yeah. Maybe I can ask my landlord to put one in."

Her soft giggle hits me. "I'm sure she'll be agreeable to that. She likes you a lot."

We slept in the next morning, a rare luxury for both of us. I woke up first, around eight, and Mila was still unconscious, curled up against me for another hour.

Mila has been at the hotel spa for the last few hours, hopefully relaxing and enjoying being pampered for once. The surprise written on her face when I walked her down and left her at the spa entrance this morning was perfect. I could tell she never had someone do this kind of thing for her before. And it makes me so fucking happy that I get to be the one to do it.

I spent the time doing my own version of relaxing, which meant a run, and then a session in the steam room before spending an hour out on our small balcony enjoying the view. This level of contented peace is unfamiliar to me, but welcome. Everything feels right in the world, as if it has all played out exactly the way it was meant to.

The hotel room door opens, and I turn to see a blissed-out Mila walk in. She drops her key card on the table, then walks over to where I'm sitting before dropping into my lap and kissing me.

"That was…The. Best. Thing. Ever." She punctuates every word with another kiss as I grin against her lips.

"Which part?"

"All of it! My skin has never felt so soft, my muscles are so relaxed, and look!" She points down at her feet, where her toes are painted a bright pink. "I think spa days should be mandatory for every woman. At least twice a year."

"Done," I say automatically. "But twice a year doesn't seem often enough. You work hard, you deserve to be pampered." My hand taps her ass lightly. "But now we gotta get going. Put on something sexy, babe. We're going out."

She jumps up with way too much energy, her excitement adorable. "Where are we going? Seriously, you need to stop spoiling me!"

I shake my head, grinning as I walk over to the closet where I've got a linen shirt and some khakis hanging up. I don't miss her appreciative stare when I take off my shorts and T-shirt.

"Think again, beautiful girl. We're getting picked up in half an hour. So get those dirty thoughts out of your head and start getting dressed."

Two hours, three wineries, and countless tastings later, we're enjoying a charcuterie picnic overlooking one of the vineyards. Everything has been perfect. We've got a case almost full of our favourite bottles from each winery. Mila hasn't stopped smiling, and neither have I.

She's leaning against me, sitting between my legs on the blanket set out on the grass for us. The late afternoon sun is warm on our skin, and her hair smells like sunshine. It's now or never. There will never be a more perfect moment to tell her how I feel.

"I know I've said this a hundred times, but thank you for bringing me here." She tips her head back to look at me. "For all of it. This has been the most magical weekend."

I lean down and kiss her.

"Jackson," she murmurs against my lips.

"Mmm?" I say, still psyching myself up to just say the three little words I want to say.

"I love you."

My head snaps back. "What? No! I was going to say it first."

Mila just laughs. "It's not a race, silly." Her hand lifts mine up in the air, and she stares at our fingers that are tangled together. "But you could still say it."

Whoops.

"I love you, Mila. Seriously, I was about to say it. I love you so damn much, sometimes it's hard to believe that a few months ago I was so determined to avoid all relationships completely. But here we are. You're in my heart, you're a part of me, and I couldn't be happier."

She turns in my lap to face me, lacing her fingers behind my neck. I press a kiss to a tear that is threatening to fall from her eye.

"Nice save." The words come out tremulous, but she's smiling.

"I love you, Mila Monroe."

The sound of someone clearing their throat interrupts us, and I look up to see the older gentleman who's been driving us around standing nearby.

"Alrighty, I hope you enjoyed your meal, but it's time for us to move on to the next winery." He must sense that he's interrupting something significant because he takes a step back. "Right. Sorry. I'll just meet you at the car. Take your time."

He backs away rapidly and I realize Mila is shaking with silent laughter, her head buried in my neck.

"Is it bad that I want to skip the last two stops and just go back to the hotel so I can show you just how much I love you?" I rumble into her ear, earning a full body shiver.

"Nope. Because I'm tempted to do the same. But there's something to be said for anticipation," comes her breathless whisper just before she stands up and starts to walk toward the car that has driven us around all afternoon. Her beauty stuns me for a second, but then she turns to look over her shoulder and stretches her arm out.

That's when I know for certain. I'll follow this woman anywhere.

# Chapter Twenty-One



*Mila*

*We did it Mom.*

My fingers run along the stainless steel counter, lined with containers ready to be filled with items for custom sandwiches. The display cases are empty but the glass sparkles with the light overhead. The entire café space is decorated in boho chic — comfortable, casual, and cozy, and different enough from the bakery side to stand out but still connected in colour scheme. Paige came through as my decorating pro, and I'm absolutely in love with how it turned out.

"This is incredible, babe." Jackson's arms come around me from behind and I let myself fall back against his chest.

"I can't believe it opens this weekend."

"I can. You're amazing, and you've worked so damn hard. Dogwood Cove's lunch scene will never be the same."

His comment is partly teasing, but I hope he's right. That was Mom's dream, and now all I can do is pray I do it justice. An incoming text on my phone beeps and interrupts my internal panic. It's my group chat with the girls, which means several more beeps immediately follow. Jackson chuckles and steps back to let me read them.

**SERENA: Just checking in to make sure Summer and Mila are still coming tonight...Just because you two are getting the D on the regular doesn't mean you get to abandon us single ladies.**

**PAIGE: Does anyone really call it the D?**

**SERENA: Those of us who aren't getting any do.**

**SUMMER: Of course I'll be there. It's book club AND we're celebrating Mila opening the café this weekend.**

**SERENA: I've got crab dip ready to go, and three bottles of wine chilling. Shit, should I grab more?**

**SUMMER: Nah, I'll bring some.**

**MILA: Guys. Of course I'll be there. And three bottles sounds like it should be enough, doesn't it?**

**PAIGE: Says the girl who went on a fancy wine tour last week.**

**MILA: Yeah...good point. Get more.**

I internally swoon, remembering my trip with Jackson. When he said he loved me, it felt like he held the key to my heart, and he finally unlocked it.

**SERENA: Okay. Enough mushy stuff. See you guys at my place tonight!!!!!!**

"What has you smiling so widely?"

I glance up at my man, the reason for my smile. "Stuff and things," I tease, sliding my hands around his waist and into his back pockets so I can give his ass a gentle squeeze. He chuckles and puts his hands on my shoulders.

"Okay, be mysterious. I have ways of getting you to talk later." He lowers his eyes suggestively and I giggle.

"I'll try to resist," I tease.

He drops a kiss to my nose. "Am I picking you up from Serena's or are you walking home?"

"That depends on how much wine we have."

His deep chuckle is followed by a squeeze of his hands. "I'll pick you up." I get one more kiss, and then Jackson turns and heads out the door. With the bakery closed for the day, I'm alone. I wander over to one of the big comfy chairs positioned by the window with a bistro table close by and sink down into it. My eyes roam over the space and another wave of gratitude mixed with disbelief and pride washes over me.

A year ago, this was nothing more than a nebulous goal, with no timeframe or thought-out plan attached to it. Now, thanks to my brother and my friends, it's a reality. I don't regret how hard I've worked or the sacrifices I've made to get here, not for a second.

And to be here, with Jackson by my side, feels absolutely surreal. Love wasn't anywhere on my radar. I never bothered to consider the possibility of somehow having it all — the career I wanted, and a relationship. It seemed impossible, made all the more evident by how many guys ran in the opposite direction as soon as they heard about my work schedule and my plans for the future.

But Jackson came out of nowhere. He is just as driven as I am, and our busy schedules and responsibilities seem to draw us closer. There is an unspoken understanding between us, a respect for what each other wants out of life, and that feels so freaking good.

Another beep comes from my phone and when I look down, I see it's Paige.

**PAIGE: Could you please bring some of Kelly's chocolate chunk cookies tonight?**

I quickly thumb out a reply and get up, heading next door to see what's left of the cookies. Once they're packaged in a box, I lock up, call Milo over to my side, and we head home.

"You need to stop smiling so much. It's creeping me out." Serena's dramatic statement makes me roll my eyes, and *not* stop smiling.

"Sorry, no can do. Here. Have another drink." I hand her the bottle of wine that's on the table beside me and with a loud huff, she refills her glass.

"Fine, but seriously, do you not realize how annoying it is having to watch you and Summer be so freaking *happy* all the time?"

Behind her teasing is a hint of Serena's vulnerable side. It's a part of her I don't think many people know about, aside from me. I know why she hasn't been on a date in five years. I catch her touching her stomach sometimes. But we don't talk about it.

I put my head on her shoulder and speak softly. "Sorry, girly. I love you, you know that, right? No matter what."

She drops her head on top of mine. "Yeah, I know. Sorry I'm being kind of a bitch. I am happy for you guys, I swear."

"Why the long faces? It's book club night!" Summer dances into the kitchen with her wine glass, interrupting us before I can reply. "Come on, Paige has our question sheets ready."

I give Serena a quick hug and we head into the other room where sure enough, Paige has our discussion questions ready and waiting.

"Is now a bad time to say I didn't get a chance to finish the book?" I wince at the glare Paige gives me.

"Yes. It is. Did you at least start it?"

"Umm, well, I planned to read it when Jackson took me away for the weekend. But we were too busy. Doing...things."

"Doing each other, you mean?" Paige quips and we all start to laugh. She's normally the most reserved of us all, so when she cracks a joke, it lands perfectly.

"Well, yeah," I say when I finally control my laughter. "Do you blame me?"

Summer lifts her glass and tips it toward me. "Not one bit. You got yourself one hot man."

"Okay, okay, well, Mila can sit the discussion out." Paige turns a pleading look to the others. "But can we go over a few of these questions, right? I tried to liven them up this month. I think you'll like them."

Curious, I lean forward and pick up one of the papers to read it over.

"Oh my God, Paige!" Serena shrieks, stomping her feet on the ground wildly. "These are awesome. Yes, girl!"

I scan the questions, my eyes widening with each one. This is...unexpected, especially coming from Paige.

Discuss the practicalities of men wearing no underwear underneath their kilt. See attached photos for examples.

Historical accuracy: Hamish and Saorise have undeniable chemistry. But in eighteenth century Scotland, would the laird's daughter really give the stable boy a blow job the first time she met him?

Location matters: sex in a barn seems common in historical romance. Would you be able to climax with a cow watching?

Anal intercourse: turn on, or turn off? Consider the scene in chapter 14 for reference.

"Umm, Paige, these are different from our usual questions," Summer says cautiously.

My eyes bounce over to Paige, who pushes her glasses up on her nose, sitting there completely composed.

"Yes, I realize that. I hoped that by adding some more salacious questions, you all might be less resistant to the discussion portion of our monthly meetings." She takes a sip of wine, and when she lowers her glass, there's a faint blush on her cheeks. "And...I decided to do some...research."

"Oh. My. God. My baby is growing up," Serena cries out as she lunges over to hug Paige.

I sit back and sip my wine, smiling at my friends going through Paige's wild questions. I don't regret not reading the book, how could I when my time was much better spent loving Jackson. But I have to admit, some of the scenes they're discussing sound....intriguing. I make a mental note to skim the book later to see if I get any inspiration for Jackson and I. Not that we need any help in the bedroom, good lord, no. But still, it could be interesting.

Opening day is here. The bakery is humming along with its usual steady stream of business, and I'm bouncing back and forth between the kitchen of the bakery and the front of the café. Hiring an entire team, including kitchen staff, to run the café was a smart choice. Baking is my passion, and if I had to spend my time in the kitchen of the café making sandwiches and soups, I'd go crazy. But today, I'm here — making sure it all runs smoothly, the food is perfect, and everyone is happy.

So far, so good.

Ethan and Summer were lucky enough to taste test with me when we were interviewing head chefs. Their moans of approval told me we made the right choice with Donna. She's a dynamo and is keeping everything in check.

There's just one thing left to do, and I need my brother here for it. When he and Summer arrive in the early afternoon, the crowd has slightly died down, even though there's still a lineup.

"Okay Mills, whatcha got?"

Summer smacks my brother lightly. "What Ethan means to say is, we're both so proud of you. This place is incredible and I just know your mom would love it."

I hug the woman I love like a sister. She knew my mom well, so for her to say that means a lot. "Thanks, Summer. I wanted you two to be the first ones to see the window art." I lead them out to the front of the café, where the window has been covered on both sides with paper. One of the waitresses is inside, ready to peel off the inner layer, revealing what is underneath.

"I know I said I was just going to keep The Nutty Muffin as the name for both places, but I decided not to do that. The café needs a name of its own, and I wanted to surprise you with it." I peel off the paper to reveal the name written across the window: Camille's.

"You named it after Mom." Ethan's voice is thick with emotion, and when I look at my older brother, I see tears pooling in his eyes. Summer's no different, except the tears are already falling. And just like that, I know I made the right decision.

I thought life couldn't get any better, but I was wrong. Everything feels perfect.

# Chapter Twenty-Two

*Jackson*

Envelopes are a thing for Mila and I now. It started with my offer from Phil to purchase half of the clinic. Then there was the weekend getaway I surprised her with. Then, on my birthday, she handed me an envelope that held the coveted bran muffin recipe inside.

I laughed when I opened it, and said it was pointless since I have her to make them for me. She didn't like that answer, but the make-up sex after was worth it.

Today I'm on my way to her house with another envelope. One that I'm hoping is the next step in the right direction for us. The letter is a fake notice to terminate my rental agreement. If she agrees for us to move in together, I'll go to Ethan and officially end my rental, since Mila wants to stay out of that situation. I get it, it's a little weird to have my girlfriend as my landlord. Easier to just think of Ethan that way. And I know we've only been officially together for a few weeks, so maybe moving in together now is moving fast, but to the rest of the world — and to my heart, it's been much longer. And I'm ready for this.

I decide to pop into the Grab N' Go grocery store to pick up some flowers. I've noticed how Mila always admires fresh flowers, but she never has them at home. She claims she works too much and isn't home enough to enjoy them. But hopefully the gesture and the sentiment are appreciated. And if not, she can always take them into the bakery.

When I'm walking to the front to check out, I suddenly hear her voice and I freeze, not wanting to be seen by her yet. I feel a little foolish, and my free hand comes up to rub the back of my neck. Thank God there's no one else here to see me being so ridiculous. Romantic things don't come naturally to me, or at least they didn't before now. There's something about her that makes me a lot more sentimental.

Of course, before I know it, I've inched my way to the front of the aisle just to see and hear her better. Every fiber of me wants to touch her; my soul craves her always. Her back is to me, and I'm about to say fuck it and just go to her when I hear what she's saying.

"...just so excited. I honestly never thought the day would come. It's going to be such a great surprise!" Her voice is full of happiness and I feel it building in me. Looks like I wasn't the only one planning a romantic surprise. But that happiness comes crashing down around me when I catch a glimpse of what she's handing the cashier.

*A box of pregnancy tests.*

My heart stops beating.

I stop breathing.

And when I do eventually draw in a breath, it's ragged and full of disbelief.

Anger wars with anguish inside of me and I honestly don't know which will win. I do know I need to get out of here, and fast. I drop the flowers on a shelf beside me and walk to the exit. The cashier, whose name I should probably know by now but can't think of in this moment, doesn't see me, she's too busy with another customer. Probably talking about Mila's big surprise.

Thank fuck this town is small enough that my house isn't too far away. I manage not to run into anyone on my way, which is a good thing because there is no fucking way I can make neighbourly small talk right now. But walking inside only makes me clench my jaw even tighter. Signs of Mila are everywhere. Her shoes are by the door, a throw blanket she decided I needed is on the couch, and memories of us infuse every inch. My chest tightens. The walls start to close in on me. I go to the back deck, but it's no better. We've talked about our pasts and our future on these chairs. We've kissed, and fucked, and loved our way around this entire property. There's no where I can go that doesn't remind me of her.

What is it about me that says, *lie to me?*

That fucking cliché repeats in my head. *Fool me once, shame on you. Fool me twice, shame on me.*

All those times we talked about our future, she made me trust her. I believed her when she said she didn't want kids, that she was happy focusing on her career and supporting me with mine. We talked about where we wanted to travel. We talked about how I would eventually take over the entire vet practice from Phil. We talked about her plans for the bakery and the café.

And all along, she was lying to me.

When Stefani told me the truth, and after I recovered from the initial shock, I realized something powerful. It wasn't so much that I grieved losing her, but rather losing the relationship I thought we had. The mutual understanding, the common goals. I decided the chances of finding a woman like that, someone who actually wanted the same things as me, were next to none, so why bother. Then she happened. Mila convinced me she was the one for me.

Which is why the pain this time feels so infinitely worse. I let myself believe that the love we had was real. And maybe it was. Unlike Stefani, who I now know never really loved me, I think Mila does. But just like Stefani, and maybe every other woman out there, she thought she could trick me into changing my life plan.

As I pace my backyard, a part of me knows I need to talk to her. I need to hear it from her. But my reaction, my pain, my anger at being betrayed again is so visceral, I can't control it right now. And despite everything, I don't want to hurt her.

Confronting her right now is a bad idea. Drinking is a good idea. Tequila. The burn might replace some of the other pain

I'm feeling. The pain in my chest, where there's an empty hole where my heart used to be. Mila took it, ripped it into shreds and burnt it in a dumpster fire.

Yeah, maybe liquor can't help that, but what the fuck do I care right now.

Four, or is it five, shots later, I'm not feeling any better. Big surprise. I go to bed, and as I lay there with the room spinning around me, all I can think is, *why?*

Waking up the next morning with the Sahara Desert in my mouth and an anvil on my head is making me regret all kinds of things. Like not finding Mila yesterday and hearing the truth from her. Like drinking too much tequila. Most of all, I regret setting myself up to be hurt like this for a second fucking time. This feels like the sort of lesson you should figure out the first time, but apparently I'm a gullible dumbass.

Lying here in bed, my hungover brain tries to come up with alternative reasons for why Mila might be excited about purchasing pregnancy tests, but I keep coming up blank. I know Ethan and Summer aren't trying, thanks to a conversation at dinner last week. Her other two friends are single, so even if it was them, there's no way they'd be excited. And sure, Mila's the kind of woman who would happily do a favour for just about anyone, but buying pregnancy tests is a personal thing. Not the kind of errand you run for just anyone.

Which is why I keep circling back to the truth I want to deny. The tests are for her.

Somehow, I manage to drag myself out of bed, but only after sending an email to Phil claiming to be sick today. He readily agrees to cover my morning appointments, and I promise to be in this afternoon. Lying to my business partner is not exactly how I wanted to enter into this relationship, but it's necessary.

Half an hour later, I'm parked in front of Mila's house. I ignored all of her messages last night asking where I was by turning my phone off. But she obviously saw me pull up, because by the time I've closed my car door, she's standing on the porch with her arms crossed in front of her.

"Good to see you're alive."

My nostrils flare, but I don't respond.

"What happened last night?" She walks down the steps, and the frustration on her face fades to concern.

The tiny part of me that is maintaining some degree of rational thought says I should at least give her a chance to explain, but seeing her, feeling my body's automatic reaction toward her is making my anger rear up stronger than ever.

I take a step back, and her brow furrows in confusion. Good. She should be confused. I sure as shit am.

"Jackson?"

"Why did you lie to me?" I ask quietly.

"What are you talking about? I didn't —"

"Yes, you *did.*" I temper my volume, aware that we're out front of her house and nosy neighbours are everywhere. "Was it all just so you could use me for something? Not that I have any fucking clue what that could be, but seriously. Was any of it true? Anything?"

"Jackson, what the hell are you talking about!" Her voice is raised, and one arm reaches out to me but I dodge it. If she touches me, I'll lose it. Just seeing her is breaking me.

"I saw you yesterday. At the store. Buying pregnancy tests. I. Saw. You."

I force myself to ignore the shock and hurt I see in her eyes.

"You've got it all wrong. Just listen to me!"

How dare she sound outraged. She has no right to be upset; I'm the one who's hurting. I'm the one with pain boiling inside of me. With my feet planted wide and my arms crossed over my body, I make my final stance.

"No. I'm done," I say harshly. But what she yells at me next makes the world fall away from beneath my feet.

"You might be, but I'm not. The tests weren't for me, Jackson. They were for Riley." She's shaking. And the words come out strangled with her own pain and anger.

*Fuck. FUCK.* Everything inside of me, all my rage, grinds to an abrupt halt. Why the hell, when I was trying to rationalize what I had seen, did I not think of Riley and Dean? I don't know them that well, but Mila's talked about them enough for me to know they're happily married, so why wouldn't they be the ones trying to conceive. The fog of hurt is lifting, leaving me with an unpleasant clarity about how badly I've fucked up.

Then my idiot brain, still in defense mode, pushes the limits by asking what turns out to be the wrong damn question.

"Why are you buying her pregnancy tests?"

If looks could kill, I would be a smouldering pile of ash right now.

"Because her car with hand controls is in the shop. She was stuck at home and didn't want to wait for Dean, she wanted to surprise him with the results. Not that *any* of that should matter. I'm allowed to do favours for my friends without worrying about you freaking out and misunderstanding things."

Shit. How the hell do I fix this? "I didn't even consider that it could be for them. Please forgive me, I messed up." The words fall flat coming out of my mouth. An apology is nowhere near enough and I know it, but my fucked up, hungover head can't think of anything to say or do right now that could make it better.

Mila puts her hand up as I step toward her. Her face is flaming red, and her eyes are filling with tears. "Stop. You don't get to come near me right now. I can't *believe* you would just jump to the conclusion that I would trick you like that, instead of just asking me what was going on. Don't you trust me?" Her voice breaks on those last words. "You need to leave, Jackson."

"Mila, no, please let me stay. Let me apologize, we can talk about this," I plead, my hand still reaching out for her. I stand there, panic rising as I see the tears start to fall and she backs away from me.

"No. I can't right now, I'm too angry at you. It's my turn. *I'm done.*"

She turns and flees inside of her house, and I hear the sound of the deadbolt locking her away from me.

That sound slams into me as the weight of my fuck up hits me and I sink to my knees right there in her front yard. For a second I debate pounding on the door and begging her to let me in, but I think better of it. She's mad, and she has every right to be mad. So instead, I stand up and stagger to my car, turning it on and driving away with barely any regard for where I'm headed.

Somehow, I end up at an empty beach, an hour or so outside of town. I sit down in the sand and stare at the waves, thinking about the last twenty-four hours and how everything went so wrong.

Mila's right, I didn't trust her. I thought I did, but I obviously didn't. Stefani's actions fucked me up, I knew that. Just like I knew I shouldn't have let myself fall for someone again so quickly. It's only been seven months, or is it eight? Either way, it clearly wasn't long enough for me to realize just how screwed up I am.

Then again, maybe no amount of time would have ever been enough. I know I overreacted to seeing Mila with the pregnancy tests. I know I should have given her the courtesy, the basic respect, to let her explain things before I freaked out. Would a few more months have allowed me to be capable of that?

The thing is, I do trust her, completely. I hate that it took losing her for me to realize, but it did. Something lifted off me in that moment when I discovered my mistake. The invisible chains around my heart that I didn't even know existed fell away, and I now know that she is it for me. I know I will never find another woman more perfect for me, more in tune with who I am and what I want out of life. She makes me happy, she makes me want to be the best person I can be, and she does it all without expecting me to change who I am.

Despite all that, despite knowing that this is all my fault, a new and painful thought comes to me. She was so quick to slam the door on me, to ignore my admittedly feeble attempt at an apology. Did what we have mean so little to her that she would toss it away after one mistake?

# Chapter Twenty-Three



I can't breathe. My lungs refuse to inhale and give me air. Eventually, survival instinct kicks in and I gasp in a breath and fight back a sob.

The accusation he just hurled at me is one thing, but for him to not even give me the damn courtesy to explain before he freaked out? No way. Not okay. How on earth could Jackson believe I would do that to him? What have I ever done to make him think for one second that he couldn't trust me? My heart hurts so deeply to realize that everything we have shared over the last few months was apparently for nothing.

After I slam and lock the door on his face, I pace around my house, steaming with emotion. Milo whines and tries to follow me until I put him on his bed and tell him to stay. He goes, but whines softly, his big soulful eyes following me.

Eventually I sink down on my couch and Milo jumps up beside me, curling into me and resting his head on my lap.

"You'll never hurt me, will you buddy?"

His tongue darts out and he licks my hand, and the tears start to fall once again. This is what I get for letting myself believe I could have it all. Apparently, I was asking for too much — to have a man who would respect me, trust me, and love me the way I deserve to be loved.

The ringing of my phone breaks through the sound of my sobs. When I look at the screen and see that it's Riley, I take several deep breaths to get control of myself.

"Hey, Riley. I hope you have good news?" Dammit. I sound stuffy from all of my tears. Hopefully she doesn't notice.

"Oh my God, Mila, I'm pregnant!"

Her obvious excitement makes me smile despite my own pain. "That is so awesome. You were right!"

Riley giggles into the phone. "I know, so crazy! I was worried I wouldn't be able to notice any differences in the beginning but man, the boob tenderness is wild!"

I laugh lightly, my happiness for her news temporarily distracting me from my heartache. "I'm so excited for you and Dean."

"Thank you so much for picking up the tests yesterday. I don't think I would have been patient enough to wait another day, and the look on Dean's face when he came home and saw the positive test on the counter was priceless."

"Mmhmm." I feel my tears starting up at her mention of the tests. God, this hurts.

"Mila? What's wrong?"

"Nothing," I try to say but it comes out as a strangled sob.

"Come on, tell me," Riley cajoles, and I break down.

"Jackson…" I sniff loudly. "Jackson saw me buying the tests and assumed they were for me. He accused me of lying to him. We had a huge fight and now I think we're over."

Riley's silent for a long moment, which is probably a good thing, because now I'm crying full-on again.

"Hang on. I don't understand. He saw you buying pregnancy tests and freaked out? Why?"

"Because his ex cheated on him and got pregnant. Because he doesn't want kids and she lied to him. Because he thinks I lied to him, too."

I know I'm barely making any sense, between my garbled explanation and my unstoppable tears, but Riley seems to grasp enough of the situation.

"Oh Mila. I'm so sorry, this is all my fault."

"No, it's not," I say adamantly. "This is Jackson's fault. Him and his stupid heart that doesn't trust me."

"But if I hadn't asked you to pick them up, none of this would have happened." Great, now Riley sounds upset, too.

"Ri, if it hadn't been this, it would have been something else. Eventually, one of us would have done something that would've freaked him out and this would've happened. He doesn't trust me, and I guess he never did. Honestly, it's probably for the best that we figured it out now." My voice sounds hollow, broken, just like my heart feels.

"Okay, so, don't get mad at me for saying this, but…" Riley's soft voice sounds hesitant, and I take a deep breath to prepare for whatever she's going to say. "Did you give him a chance to apologize? If he's been lied to before about this kind of thing, maybe he needs a little more understanding about why it's hard for him."

"He didn't give me a chance to explain before he accused me," I cry.

"Okay, okay. Never mind," Riley says, placating my frustration.

But I have to admit, she's got a point that I'm starting to realize might be valid. Yeah, he should have tried asking me for the truth instead of making an assumption. But I also could have given him a chance to properly apologize before slamming the door in his face.

"Why don't you give each other some space, then maybe talk again when you've calmed down?"

I sigh. "Thanks, Riley. I'm sorry to dump all over your good news like that. I really am happy for you."

"I know you are. And I *am* sorry that your favour to me created this mess."

"Don't apologize, please. This mess is no one's fault but mine and Jackson's."

"I hope you guys figure it out," she says softly.

It takes me a minute, but eventually I reply, "Me too."

One of the downsides to owning my own business is how diffi-cult it is to swing time off. And with the café newly opened, it's extra complicated. But when I tell Kelly I need some personal time, she doesn't bat an eye, even after recently covering for me when Jackson took me away for the weekend. A cryptic phone call to Summer is all it takes, and I've got one of her beachfront cabins to myself for a night. I have a sneaky suspicion she and the girls will show up at some point to find out what's going on, especially since I admitted to Summer that I would be here by myself, but at least for now it's just me, Milo, and the beach.

It's been twenty-four hours, give or take, since my fight with Jackson. The time has given me a chance to calm down a little and acknowledge just how much I overreacted to *his* overre-action. I guess two people who didn't want a relationship in the first place aren't the best communicators. The bottom line is, I love him, even if he did accuse me of something I would never even consider doing. Even if he does clearly still have some unresolved trust issues, thanks to his bitch of an ex. Even if he did fumble and fail at attempting to apologize. Although, if I'm being really honest, that last one is just as much my fault for closing the door on his face.

As I watch my goofy dog frolic in the waves, I pull my sweater tighter around my body. There's definitely a chill in the air as fall makes itself known. If Jackson were here, he'd wrap his arms around me, or give me his sweater, or find me a blanket. Whatever it would take to make me comfortable, he would do it. He's kind, thoughtful, generous, and loving.

And he made a mistake.

Because he's human.

When I hear a car door slam behind me my heart jumps. But it's not him. I stand up, brushing sand off my pants as Summer, Paige, and Serena come down the beach toward me. They've all got bags in their arms, and I can guess what's inside.

"We're crashing your pity party, or whatever this is," Summer calls out.

"And getting stupid drunk," Serena adds.

"Don't worry, I brought plenty of food." Pragmatic as always, Paige's contribution makes me smile gratefully at her.

When they reach me, all three of them drop their loads to the ground and fold me in to a group hug. "Everything is a mess, you guys," I say, my words muffled by Serena's shoulder.

"That's okay. If we can fix this place up, we can fix whatever happened," Summer says as we pull apart. We spend the next few minutes getting settled and making up a giant pitcher of sangria. Summer drags out one of the propane firepits, a necessity during the dry summers and a nice convenience when you don't have the energy to build a real fire. Once we're all settled with drinks in hand around the flickering flames, I know it's time to come clean.

"Okay. Before I tell you how it all went wrong, I need each of you to promise me you won't be mad." I look at each of them in turn, and they all nod. "When Jackson and I first started dating," I say with air quotes around the d-word, "It was all fake. He needed to show Doctor Morton that he was serious and committed to the town for more than just his job, and I wanted to get all of you to back off from giving me a hard time about being such a workaholic. We figured a quick and easy fake relationship for a few months would do the trick."

I pause partly to take a long drink of sangria, and partly to give them all a chance to process that. Serena's the first one to react.

"I don't buy it. I saw you guys at the bar that night, *before* you even said you were dating, and there was no way you were faking that insane chemistry. He orbited around you like you were the freaking sun."

Summer's voice is laced with disappointment. "So all of those dinners with Ethan and I were what? Fake?"

I nod slowly, hating that I've clearly hurt my closest friends. "At first. And guys, look, I'm sorry. I hated lying to you, but I was so sick of hearing the comments about how much I work, and how I needed to have more fun."

"You could have just told us how you felt." Paige's quiet voice confirms that she's also upset by what I've revealed. I turn to her, hoping I can appeal to her logical side and then get the others to forgive me.

"I know I could have, and I should have. But it wasn't just about me. Jackson needed it to stay secret as well. The only reason Riley knew is because she overheard us talking one morning at the bakery."

"Wait, Riley knew?" Serena interrupts.

"Yeah, but not on purpose. Like I said, she heard us one morning and questioned me about it. I'm really sorry, I never wanted to hurt you."

It's not lost on me that here I am, asking for forgiveness from my best friends the same way Jackson tried to ask for my forgiveness yesterday. Hopefully, these girls are more willing to give it to me than I was to him.

After several tense, silent moments, Summer is the one to finally speak.

"I don't like it, but I get it. And at the end of the day, we love you, even when you do stupid things like keep secrets from us. And I'm sorry we ever made you feel uncomfortable about how you choose to live your life. That's not fair."

"I concur. Thank you, Summer, for saying it so well. Mila, you are absolutely forgiven, and I, too, apologize for anything I may have said that contributed to this decision."

"Thanks Paige," I say, smiling at her.

"I don't buy it. Let's go back to your *at first* comment." Serena's foot is bouncing against her leg, and she's still got a wary look in her eyes. I knew she would be the hardest to win over.

"So, we started as friends, fake dating. Then we...hooked up."

"Ah ha! I knew there was chemistry!" Serena pumps her arm in the air, then looks back at me. "But there's more, isn't there?"

"Yeah, lots more. We did the whole friends with bene-fits-slash-fake dating thing for a while, but Jackson was worried it would get messy, so we stopped having sex. In retrospect, it was smart, because we both were starting to develop real feelings."

"Why would that be a bad thing?" Summer asks and I shrug.

"Because neither one of us wanted an actual relationship. He was hurt, badly, by his ex-fiancée, and I didn't think I had the time, or that I would ever find a guy who could appreciate how committed I am to the bakery and the café." I take another long sip of sangria, as my thoughts flit over all the ways Jackson is so right for me. "But he did. He got it. He's committed to his career, and we want the same things in life, short term and long term. So eventually we decided to try being together for real."

"Okay, that actually sounds kinda romantic. Ooh, we should read a fake dating book next month."

I fix Summer with a look. "You might want to hear the rest first."

Summer's eyes widen, and she takes a sip of sangria. I do the same, and then another. This is the part that hurts.

"What I have to tell you is not exactly my news to share, so please keep it quiet. But you need to understand the whole story. You know that Riley and Dean are trying to get pregnant." They all nod. "Well, two days ago she asked me to pick up a box of tests for her. Her car was in the shop, and she wanted to surprise Dean if it was positive, so she didn't want to ask him to pick the tests up. Of course, I was happy to, and didn't think twice. But Jackson saw me buying them."

I close my eyes at the pain that comes from remembering how angry he was when he accused me of trying to trick him like his ex did. I know that anger was masking a deeper pain, but that doesn't make it any easier.

"Why would that matter?" Paige asks, her voice quiet but curious.

"Because his ex lied to him their entire relationship, saying she didn't want kids either. But the truth was, she figured she could either force him to have kids or convince him to change his mind. And when she realized that wasn't going to happen, she cheated on him and got pregnant with another man's baby. While they were still technically engaged."

Three simultaneous gasps of shock rise up around me. But I ignore them and push on through.

"Yesterday he showed up at my house and accused me of doing the same thing. He didn't ask why I was buying the tests, he just assumed I was like his ex and freaked out. I told him they were for Riley, he tried to give me some half-assed apology, and I shut the door in his face. Which brings us to now." I gesture with my arms at my face, puffy from crying, red rimmed eyes, greasy hair, and generally miserable appearance. "He fucked up, I overreacted, and now I don't know if we're together or not, if he trusts me or not, or whether I can forgive him."

For the second time, silence falls over our group. This time, it's Paige who finally says something.

"Do you love him?"

I nod, feeling those damn tears burning again.

"Then you forgive him. You work together to communicate better, you focus on his trust issues and your defensive reaction issues, and you figure it out."

The way she says it, so cut and dry just like always makes sense. It doesn't sound easy, but it sounds like the only way forward.

"I know you're right. But...can we still get drunk tonight and stay here?" I ask softly, looking down at my drink. "I'm not ready to see him yet."

Because the truth is, there's a chance that even if he wants to apologize, Jackson might *not* want to try and move on from this together. And I'm not ready to face that possibility yet.

# Chapter Twenty-Four

*Jackson*

Thirty-six hours and I still don't have a fucking clue how I'm going to fix things with Mila. I made it through my day at the clinic with no questions from anyone about why I had to come in late, or why I looked like shit.

Now I'm back at home, eyeing the bottle of tequila. Yeah, I know, I should learn from last time. It didn't solve anything.

Suddenly there's a pounding on my door, followed by Ethan's voice barking out my name. Well, shit. I guess he knows what went down.

I go to the door, widening my stance to brace myself before opening it. Sure enough, the first thing that comes flying through is Ethan's fist, straight to my stomach.

"That's for hurting my sister and believing for even a second that she would screw you over."

I groan, doubled over, but manage to nod my head. "Yeah, man. I deserve that." Slowly I make my way upright and look him in the eye. "I fucked up. I let my past freak me out, and I made a very wrong assumption. I want to make it right, trust me."

Ethan levels me with a glare. "Exactly how do you plan on doing that?"

My hand comes up to run through my hair. "I have no fucking idea." I turn to walk back inside. "You want a beer?"

Ethan follows me into the kitchen, I hand him a bottle, and we go to the back deck. We sit in tense silence for a few minutes, drinking our beer, staring out at the empty yard. Harley comes out, winds his way between our feet, then heads back inside. No sunshine for him to lie in means he's not hanging out. Eventually, Ethan looks over at me with a solemn expression.

"I won't apologize for punching you."

"I don't expect you to. I deserved it."

"But I might be able to help you fix this."

I turn to face him, surprised by his offer. "Why would you do that?"

Ethan takes a long pull from his beer before answering. "Because she was happy with you. Happier than I've seen her in a long time. You helped her find balance in life, showed her there was more than just the bakery and her friends. She needs you." Once again, his eyes turn to mine with laser focus. "And I think you need her."

I nod, slowly. "I do." Another minute of silence passes between us, but this time it's a lot less tense. "Is she...do you know how she's doing?" I ask cautiously.

"Yeah, she's fine. The girls are with her, they're having a girls night down at the resort."

"Good. That's good."

Ethan sets down his empty beer bottle and claps his hands on the top of his legs. "Alright, so listen. Here's what I suggest…"

By the time Ethan leaves, we've got a solid plan for how I'm going to ask Mila for a second chance. It involves a lot of groveling and a lot of sugar. And sharing one of my secrets in hopes of earning her trust again. That part Ethan doesn't know about, however.

This morning Ethan and Reid are back over at my house, but this time I'm not greeted with a punch to the gut.

"Okay, let's get baking," Reid says, lifting the tray of coffees he's carrying over his head. "I had to lie to Mila at the bakery this morning when she asked why I wasn't dressed to go to the school, so this had better work. I don't use my flex hours for just any old reason, you know."

I clap my hand on his shoulder and take a coffee from him gratefully. "Thanks, man. I really appreciate you and Ethan helping, fuck knows I'm not the best baker."

"Neither are we," Ethan replies wryly. "Let's just hope I've watched my sister often enough that we can follow a recipe."

"And you're sure this is her favourite?" I ask, checking the recipe he emailed me last night to make sure I haven't forgotten anything.

"Yup. German Chocolate Cake is her ultimate favourite. She doesn't make it for the bakery so that she's not tempted to eat it all the time, that's how much she loves it. She says it's the only thing that's irresistible for her."

"Perfect."

Yeah, right. I spoke too soon. Looking around my kitchen an hour later, and it literally looks as if a grocery store puked up the entire baking aisle across the countertops.

"Umm, so, the caramel layer goes next, then the coconut?" Reid asks, looking at me, confused.

"No, no, no. The coconut goes *in* the caramel stuff." Ethan takes over, stirring the bowl in front of Reid. "You start grating the chocolate shavings for the top."

I'm carefully leveling chocolate cake, only half paying attention to what the guys are saying. Aside from the mess, things have gone surprisingly well. We only burnt one batch of coconut that was toasting in the oven, the cakes turned out perfectly, and that caramel stuff is fucking delicious.

Eventually the cake is done. Leaning slightly to the side, but done. The three of us stand back and examine it critically.

"You didn't level them."

"No shit. It was hard," I reply, shoving Reid with my shoulder. "You had the easy job."

"Should've used a level," mutters Ethan.

"At least we know it should taste good," Reid reasons, and I let out a sigh of relief.

"Yeah. Hopefully it works."

Ethan walks over, opens the dishwasher and starts to load it. "It'll help, but you better be prepared to grovel."

I join him. "Trust me, I am. As long as the cake softens her up so she'll listen to me this time."

I see Ethan wince.

"Yeah, so, about that. Remember I told you when we were working on the café that she's got reasons for being wary of relationships? Well, I'm guessing her reaction to your fuck up is because of that. It's not my story to tell, but Mila's got good reason to be defensive. Just give her the space to figure that out."

"I can do that."

I can, and I will. I'll do whatever it takes to get her back.

Standing on her porch, I'm the most nervous I've ever been. I'm holding onto the plate carrying the lopsided cake with a death grip, contemplating how to ring the doorbell, when it opens and Mila looks at me, confused.

"Why are you just standing there?" Her eyes drop down, then widen when she sees the cake. "Is that...did you bake?"

I thrust it into her hands. "It's a German Chocolate Cake. Your favourite."

She takes it, and when I see a cautious smile cross her face, my shoulders relax.

"You made me a cake."

"Yeah. Ethan and Reid helped." My voice is gruff, thick with emotion. I want to touch her so badly. I want her to invite me in and let me fix this. I miss her. I miss us. Mila looks at me for a moment, her eyes studying me. Then they soften, and she steps back to let me in.

"Guess we better try a piece."

I step inside, and Milo comes ambling up to me, sniffing my legs before nudging and licking my hand. I give him a pet, then follow Mila into the kitchen.

We both sit down at the table, our chairs facing each other. Mila slices the cake and pours us each a glass of milk to go with it. When I raise my eyebrows at her choice of beverage she shrugs. "Trust me." As soon as the words leave her mouth, her eyes widen, and she casts an uncertain glance my way.

"I do trust you." I say quietly, hoping the truth behind those words gets through to her.

She nods thoughtfully. "Do you see how that was hard for me to believe when you came here accusing me without bothering to ask the truth?" She says it all so calmly, as if she isn't talking about the single worst conversation I've had with a woman, ever, even including the day Stefani confessed to me.

"I do. I know I was a completely misguided idiot to jump to conclusions like that. It wasn't fair, it was disrespectful, and immature. But it wasn't that I don't, or didn't, trust you. I just freaked out and let my past completely colour my perception of things."

"I'm not her, Jackson."

I can't hold back any longer. I take her hand in mine, threading my fingers through hers and lifting it to my lips to press a kiss to her knuckles. "God, I know that, Mila. You are nothing like her. You're the woman I need, the woman I want, and the only woman worth fighting for."

She leans down and kisses our hands right over top of where I kissed them. "Good line, Doctor Holt." When she looks back up at me, her eyes glisten with what I hope are happy tears. I shift forward in my seat just slightly, wanting her to close the distance. When she does, it's as if my soul breathes a sigh of relief. Our lips touch, lightly at first. Then with a moan, Mila takes it deeper. My lips drink in the feel of her as I pull her into my lap. She straddles my legs and presses herself against me.

"I missed you," I mutter against her mouth, loving the fact that I feel her lips curve up into a smile. I reluctantly pull back. "Wait. As much as I want to just keep kissing you, I have to tell you something."

She shifts back on my legs with a sigh. "Yeah, same here."

"You go first."

Mila arches her eyebrow at me, but doesn't argue. "Fine. I wanted to apologize. I should have remembered what you've been through, and thought about how that might affect your reaction to seeing me buying Riley's pregnancy tests. And when you tried to apologize, I shouldn't have shut the door in your face. I was just so angry, and so hurt."

"Ethan said you have a reason for being defensive," I say cautiously. At her frown, I hurry to continue. "He didn't tell me what that was; he said it was your story to tell. But I'm hoping you will tell me, so I can understand."

Mila drops her head down on my shoulder, turning to bury her face in my neck. I twist to press a kiss to her head, and just wait.

"My last serious boyfriend, well, as serious as they ever were, was a real asshole. We were only together for a few months, but that was a long time for me. It's not that I have a problem with commitment or anything, it's just that no guy was ever good enough for me to keep around." Her voice trails off and I feel her arms squeeze tighter around me. "Until you."

Fuck, I want to kiss her when she says that, but I don't. I do start to run my hand up and down her back, hoping to give her comfort and strength to say whatever she needs to say.

"So anyway, this ex, Derek, he was really insecure. Always needed me to reassure him that I liked him, that kind of stupid stuff. We were young; I was only twenty, he was twenty-two. But I always felt like I had to defend myself to him. He wasn't controlling or anything, just insecure about everything. Questioning why I was going out, who I would be with, why I wouldn't go out with him. I shouldn't have bothered staying with him as long as I did in retrospect. The final straw was when he came over and flew off the handle at me when he found the condoms he had brought over previously, the box open and half empty. He started yelling and accused me of cheating on him. The truth was, I had moved some of them into the bedside drawer so we wouldn't have to get up and go to the bathroom to get them. It was so stupid, and he freaked out. I kicked him out right away. There was no way I could be with someone who didn't trust me, not to mention someone who would overreact like that."

"And then I did something stupidly similar," I finish for her. "Jesus, Mila, I can't tell you how sorry I am. But I swear to you, my reaction had everything to do with my shit and nothing to do with you."

"I know that. Just like my reaction was about my past and not you." Without warning, Mila leans in and kisses me, hard and fast. "Here's the thing, Jackson, we're both human. Which means we're going to fuck up sometimes. But I love you, and that means I'm committed to working through the fuck ups and learning to do better. So, I accept your apology if you accept mine, and I promise not to get defensive and overreact next time you try to apologize for whatever stupid thing you might do. Although, not doing anything stupid would be even better."

I let out a relieved chuckle at that. "Deal. And I love you, too, Mila Monroe. So fucking much. Thank you for giving me another chance."

She cocks her head and gives me a sexy, sassy smile. "You can thank me with orgasms."

I stand up with her in my arms. "Don't have to tell me twice."

# CHAPTER TWENTY-FIVE

*Mila*

I laugh as Jackson carries me down the hall to my room, closing the door on poor, confused Milo.

"Did we just get over our first fight?" I ask, twisting the hair at the nape of his neck around my finger.

"Yeah, babe. We did. It was a fucking doozy of a fight, too; let's make that our first and *last* one." Jackson sets me down beside the bed. My hands instantly go to the hem of his shirt and I lift it up and over his head.

"Not likely. Have you met me? I'm a stubborn girl."

He shakes his head slowly, and the glowing fire in his eyes melts away the last of the icy grip that has been around my heart for the last two days. "Not stubborn. Strong, independent, fierce, committed..."

I interrupt him with a kiss. "Stop, you're making me blush." He laughs, kisses me, then keeps going.

"Perfect, amazing, beautiful, kind, generous, sexy, and most importantly, mine."

"Well, when you put it that way," I return his kiss, taking it deeper. Then I let my lips trail down his torso, over the ripples of his stomach, following the small trail of hairs that leads to where I want to be. Unzipping his pants, I pull them down with his underwear. The second his cock is free, I wrap my hand around it and tug gently.

"Fuck, babe," he groans, his hand going to the back of my head. "I thought I was going to be the one handing out orgasms."

I swipe my tongue over the bead of pre-cum glistening on his tip. "You'll get your turn. But first, I need to say thank you for being so understanding and forgiving."

Jackson bends down, his eyes brimming with love as he cups my chin. "There's nothing to forgive." He kisses me, then straightens. "But feel free to do what you were going to do anyway."

I giggle and give him an exaggerated eye roll before returning my attention to what is in front of me. I lick my lips, earning another groan. Keeping my eyes fixed on his, my mouth opens and takes the first inch of him in, sucking and swirling my tongue around him. I start to slide up and down his length, still keeping my mouth at the tip.

"Fuuuuck." He expels the word as a long sigh when I finally slide him in my mouth as far as I can take him. Slowly I begin to move up and down, taking my time alternating between squeezing with my hand and licking long, slow licks along his cock. I slide my hand around from his hip, to cup his balls and give them an experimental tug.

"Jesus Christ!"

I do it again, humming with pleasure when his hand tightens in my hair.

"Oh God. Mila. Babe. I'm gonna come." He gently pulls me off and lifts me up, capturing my mouth in a deep kiss. "I need to be inside of you." He walks the few steps over to the bed and sits down, pulling me into his lap. I push on his chest so that he lays down, and somehow he uses his strong arms to shift us both backward so that we're fully on the bed. I never liked being manhandled by guys, but with Jackson it's fucking sexy. I stretch out on top of him, bringing our bodies into total contact. His hand drifts down to squeeze my ass, sending a fresh wave of wet heat between my legs.

"I need you," I moan against his lips. Grabbing my hips, he lifts me up slightly, and lines me up with his cock. I sit up, and slide down his shaft, gasping at the fullness of having him inside of me. We both still, connected by our bodies and our eyes. Slowly my hips start to rock back and forth, creating a delicious friction as my pelvis grinds against him. It's not enough, though, I need more. My hand snakes down to play with my clit, but Jackson covers it with his own hand.

"Mine." It comes out as more of a growl than a word, and good grief is that hot. I let him thumb my clit as my body undulates on top of him. My hands cup my breasts, squeezing them, then run up to thread through my hair. When I feel my muscles tightening, readying for what's sure to be an explosive release, I drop my hands to place them on his chest and use the leverage to lift up and down more vigorously, chasing the orgasm that's coiling inside of me.

"Jackson, more. I need more."

He grabs my hips, his fingers digging into my ass as he lifts me up and down, guiding my movements.

"I want to give you everything."

I come apart as he squeezes my ass one more time and my hips grind over him. He pulls me down into a sloppy, hot, deep kiss. I feel him thrust up into me a few times and then he's groaning into my mouth and I feel him shoot off inside of me. I collapse down into his waiting arms, feeling his heart pounding in time with my own. Our skin is slick with sweat, and I kiss his chest, tasting the saltiness of him.

"I love you."

"I love you, too." He kisses the top of my head, leaving his lips pressed against my hair for several seconds. "You're everything, babe. You are the love of my life. And I never want to stop loving you." His voice is full of emotion, and I lift my head, seeking his lips. We stay like that, kissing, our hands roaming over each other's bodies, touching and exploring every inch. Even though it's only the afternoon, I feel myself relaxing so fully, my eyes are drifting closed.

"Sleep, babe," Jackson whispers. I nuzzle into his chest and give in to the pull of sleep.

I wake up some time later to an empty bed. But I can hear Jackson talking to Milo, and the sound of his deep voice makes me smile. I stretch, and climb out of bed, grabbing a T-shirt and panties to wear. When I get to the kitchen, Jackson is playing with Milo, wearing only a pair of sweatpants that he left over here a few weeks ago.

Holy crap on a cracker. That man, wearing nothing but low-slung sweats, loving on my dog. It just does not get hotter than that.

"Are you just gonna stand there drooling, or are you going to come here and let me love you?"

I startle, not realizing he saw me watching him. He's smirking at me, but his eyes widen when he takes in what I'm wearing. I arch my brow at him and place my hand on my hip. "Now who's drooling?"

He stands up and prowls over to me. "You're wearing next to nothing. Of course I'm going to drool."

"You're the one wearing sex pants."

"Sex pants?"

I gesture to his perfectly defined abs and hips on full display, thanks to those pants. And of course, the imprint of his magnificent cock. He's obviously going commando under there and the thought of tugging down his pants and freeing him makes me bite my lip in anticipation.

"Yeah. Sex pants. Pants that make me, or hell, any woman, think of sex."

His hands slide around my hips, going under my shirt to find my bare skin. "So, you're thinking of sex right now?" He drops his voice down low. "Like, right, right now?"

I look up at him and nod slowly. Then without warning, his hands go around me, and I'm lifted up and into the air, tossed over his shoulder, and I'm carried back to the bedroom.

"Oh my God, Jackson!" He just chuckles and squeezes my ass, which is hanging out, thanks to my lack of clothes.

"What? I need to live up to my sex pants, don't I?

Even though he can't see me, I roll my eyes, even as I'm grinning with anticipation.

And boy, does he ever live up to those pants. Over and over again.

**

When my alarm goes off the next morning, my eyes fly open. Even though my body is stiff in ways I never imagined possible, I'm happy. We barely slept last night, too busy making love over and over. He gave me an incredible orgasm in the tub, then I returned the favour in bed — this time swallowing every last drop. But then, when he slid into me for the final time before we finally fell asleep, it was so sweet and slow, full of tender love. I came close to crying when I climaxed, feeling the wash of loving warmth cover us both.

I sneak out of bed, leaving Jackson sleeping. But as I'm mixing up protein shakes for both of us — yeah, he managed to get me hooked on starting my day with one — his arms snake around me, tugging me back into the wall of muscled heat that is his body.

"Morning, babe." He kisses my shoulder, his voice still rough with sleep.

I turn in his arms, looping mine around his neck. "Hi. You can go back to sleep if you want, come in for breakfast later."

He blinks his eyes fully open and shakes his head. "No way. You're up, I'm up, remember? Can I keep you company at the bakery?"

"Of course," I smile. "But I need to leave in ten minutes. So you better get that fine ass of yours dressed."

His low chuckle fills me with happiness as he goes back to the bedroom. As I start to gather all of my things, I see an envelope sitting underneath his wallet, where he must have left them yesterday. I pull it out; it's blank.

"Open it."

I look up to see him pulling on his shirt, and looking at me with a mixture of hope, love, and excitement.

"I was on my way to give you that when I saw you at the store," he says, wincing. "Kind of ruined the mood. But I'm hoping you'll accept it now."

I slide open the envelope and unfold the letter inside. Scanning it quickly, I feel my face stretch into a smile.

"You want to move out of your house."

He nods.

"Where are you planning on living?" I know the answer, at least I hope I know what the answer is, but I want to hear it from him. He walks over and takes my hands.

"Well, seeing as I don't want to be apart from you another night, and seeing as our pets are friends, and your house is closer to both our jobs, I was kind of hoping I might move in here."

My damn eyes start leaking again. "That's sort of presumptuous of you, isn't it?"

Now he's smiling and lifting our hands up so he can kiss my knuckles. "Not presumptuous if I'm just moving us in the direction that we're already headed."

"But think of the rumours that will fly when people know we're living together." Now I'm just messing with him; the truth is, I already have a key for him.

"Ah, but think of the romance. Think of *our* romance."

I lean to the side, open a drawer, and pull out his key. Dangling it in front of him, I can't hold back my grin.

"Hey Jackson, want to move in with me?"

"I thought you would never ask."

I'm late getting to the bakery, and for the first time, I really don't care.

# Epilogue

*Jackson*

Small towns really do Christmas differently. At least, Dogwood Cove does. All of the store fronts on main street are decorated, and the giant tree next to the gazebo is all lit up. Mila roped me into helping her serve cookies and hot chocolate at the tree lighting event, and I have to admit, it was pretty special to see everyone together, bundled up against the cold, singing Christmas songs.

There's no snow, but that's typical for here. It's just cold and wet most days. Even Milo doesn't love going out for walks — that is, he didn't until I bought him a jacket to wear. Yeah, I bought my girlfriend's dog a jacket.

When Mila told me there would be a live nativity, I laughed at her. Then she said she was serious. Apparently, the Martin family farm has a petting zoo, along with Christmas trees that you can cut down yourself, and each year they bring some animals to participate in a live nativity scene. I honestly can't comprehend what that even means, but Phil reassured me the animals are all happy to participate. Seeing as he has almost completely taken over as the large animal vet for the area, he would know best.

We're meeting Ethan, Summer, Paige, Serena, Reid, and Ethan's friend, Finn, who just moved to town, at the bakery tonight, then walking over to the nativity together.

When Finn walks through the door, he looks...disheveled, to say the least. I don't know the guy well, but even I can see he's not himself.

"Hey man, what the hell happened to you?" Ethan asks.

"Don't. Ask." Finn clips out. "Mila, tell me you've got that bottle of peppermint schnapps we stashed here last year. If I can't have boozy hot chocolate tonight, I'm going home."

She gives him a look but goes into the back and comes out with a bottle. He reaches out for it, but she holds it back.

"Are you getting drunk to avoid something, forget something, or accept something?"

"How about all three?" he replies grimly, and Mila hands it over before coming back to my side. My arm automatically wraps around her.

I tune out the conversation around us, Ethan grilling Finn, trying to get details out of him. As I have so many times over the last several months, my thoughts are filled with the woman in my arms. She turns to face me, and her hands slide into my back pockets and squeeze gently. My eyes darken as I look down at her impish smile.

"What are you doing, woman?"

She lifts up on her toes and whispers in my ear. "Just warming my hands up."

"I'll warm you up plenty, later," I rumble back, kissing her neck.

"Hey, you two, save the lovey-dovey stuff for when we're not around, would you?" Serena's sarcastic voice makes me smile against Mila's skin but I don't move, nuzzling her until she pushes me away laughing.

"Sorry, Serena," she tries to say, but my hand comes up to cover her mouth. When I lift it away, I replace it with my mouth.

"Nope, not sorry. Won't apologize for loving you."

"Ah, fuck. Now you're being all swoony and romantic," Serena moans. "Finn, hand over the schnapps."

I chuckle and step around Mila so I'm behind her, and pull her against my chest. "Better?"

Serena nods vigorously. "Yep. Better. I can handle that level of PDA. Any more and I'm out. It was bad enough when it was just Ethan and Summer, but having two smoochy couples around is too much."

"Serena, be happy for our friends," Paige chides as she walks up with a cup of hot chocolate in her hand. "But I'll take some schnapps as well, please. Perhaps a slight buzz will alleviate the loneliness we single people are inclined to feel around the holiday season."

"That doesn't exactly make me feel better," Serena mutters, but she hands over the bottle.

Ethan raises his voice as the girls debate how much schnapps to add. "Okay, I have to go and give a speech, then this crazy thing can get started."

We all troop outside as a group, laughing and joking together. It hits me that I not only found love here. I've found a home, friends, and a life that makes me happy. And it's all thanks to Mila. My heart grows even more full of love for her, and I tip her chin up so I can kiss her.

"What's that for?"

I smile down at her. "Nothing. Just needed to kiss you." She smiles back, and leans into my arms.

"I love you."

And I will never get tired of hearing *that*.

The live nativity surprises me, in that I actually really enjoy it. I have to admit, seeing live animals interacting with the people pretending to be angels and shepherds makes me laugh. Kids are petting the cows, and there is a random goat running around gently headbutting everyone. It's quaint, funny, and something you could only pull off in a place like Dogwood Cove. Seeing Mila's eyes light up as she loves on all of the animals is pretty amazing. Just when I think she can't get any more perfect for me, she does.

And if anyone else notices how Reid keeps staring over at Abigail Martin, who is handling the animals tonight, they don't say a word. If he thinks he's being subtle, he's wrong. The guy needs some lessons in how to not be obvious about your attraction to a woman. Hell, I hid my true feelings about Mila long enough, maybe I could help him.

It feels like an eternity before the evening's events are over and Mila and I are walking home. There's a peaceful stillness tonight. It's the kind of evening where you just know nothing bad can happen to you. And when we get home, to our house, we walk in the door to see our pets cuddled up together on Milo's giant dog bed.

Mila leans her head down on my shoulder with a soft sigh. "Is it just me, or is our life freaking perfect?"

I kiss the top of her head, thinking I couldn't have put it better myself.

"It's perfect for us, babe. And that's all that matters."

**Want a peek into Mila and Jackson's future? Get their bonus scene by visiting https://bit.ly/JuliaJarrett_RR_bonus**

# ACKNOWLEDGEMENTS

This story has been bouncing in my head ever since I wrote Always and Forever. But it would never have made it to life if it weren't for the encouragement of my team - Erica, Erin, and Chris. The support of the best author friends a girl could ask for - Mae, Chelle, Georgia and Claire. And of course, the patient understanding of my husband and kids!

And, the biggest thank you goes to you my readers. You've embraced my Canadian roots, and fallen in love with Dogwood Cove and everyone who exists there. and I could not possibly be more grateful.

# Also By Julia Jarrett

### **Dogwood Cove**

Always and Forever

Rumours and Romance

Work and Play

Truth and Temptation

Then and Now

Passion and Promises: A Dogwood Cove Novella Collection

### **The Donnellys of Dogwood Cove**

Dare To Kiss you

Hate To Want You

Pretend To Love You

Promise To Marry You

Dare To Marry You: A Donnellys of Dogwood Cove Holiday
Novella

One Night To Win You

### **Standalone**

Seductive Swimmer - A standalone novel set in the Cocky Hero World, inspired by Vi Keeland and Penelope Ward's Cocky Bastard series

# About The Author

Julia Jarrett is a busy mother of two boys, a happy wife to her real-life book boyfriend and the owner of two rescue dogs, one from Guatemala and another one from Taiwan. She lives on the West Coast of Canada and when she isn't writing contemporary romance novels full of relatable heroines and swoon-worthy heroes, she's probably drinking tea (or wine) and reading.

For a complete listing of Julia Jarrett books please visit www.authorjuliajarrett.com/books

**<u>Follow Julia:</u>**

Instagram @juliajarrettauthor

Facebook Reader Group: Julia Jarrett's Nutty Muffins

TikTok @julia.jarrett.author